Acting Edition

Bleachers

by Noah Haidle

FOR PRODUCTION INQUIRIES
UNITED STATES AND CANADA
info@concordtheatricals.com
1-866-979-0447
UNITED KINGDOM AND EUROPE
licensing@concordtheatricals.co.uk
020-7054-7298

Each title is subject to availability from Concord Theatricals Corp., depending upon country of performance. Please be aware that *BLEACHERS* may not be licensed by Concord Theatricals Corp. in your territory. Professional and amateur producers should contact the nearest Concord Theatricals Corp. office or licensing partner to verify availability.

No one shall make any changes in this title(s) for the purpose of production. No part of this book may be reproduced, stored in a retrieval system, scanned, uploaded, or transmitted in any form, by any means, now known or yet to be invented, including mechanical, electronic, digital, photocopying, recording, videotaping, or otherwise, without the prior written permission of the publisher. No one shall share this title(s), or any part of this title(s), through any social media or file hosting websites.

For all inquiries regarding motion picture, television, online/digital and other media rights, please contact Concord Theatricals Corp.

MUSIC AND THIRD-PARTY MATERIALS USE NOTE

Licensees are solely responsible for obtaining formal written permission from copyright owners to use copyrighted music and/or other copyrighted third-party materials (e.g. artworks, logos) in the performance of this play and are strongly cautioned to do so. If no such permission is obtained by the licensee, then the licensee must use only original music and materials that the licensee owns and controls. Licensees are solely responsible and liable for clearances of all third-party copyrighted materials, including without limitation music, and shall indemnify the copyright owners of the play(s) and their licensing agent, Concord Theatricals Corp., against any costs, expenses, losses and liabilities arising from the use of such copyrighted third-party materials by licensees. For music, please contact the appropriate music licensing authority in your territory for the rights to any incidental music.

IMPORTANT BILLING AND CREDIT REQUIREMENTS

If you have obtained performance rights to this title, please refer to your licensing agreement for important billing and credit requirements.

CHARACTERS

THE TUBA SECTION

ELIZA – Fifteen. Second chair. A rebel.

NEIL – Seventeen. Third chair. A budding philosopher possibly from another dimension.

JOY – Sixteen. First chair. A leader.

RUSTY – Fourteen. Fourth chair. Scared.

CHORUS

Optional and expandable, the Chorus are silent witnesses, musical ghosts, mascots who never get to take their helmet off, stagehands who never take the stage. They can march, freeze, hum, or shadow the main cast during transitions.

SETTING

Your high school bleachers.

TIME

The high school football season.

AUTHOR'S NOTES

Have you ever heard of that movie *American Pie*?

Have you ever heard a joke that starts, "This one time, at band camp…"

(I would ask, "Do you remember…" but most of the people reading this were born long after the film came out in 1999.)

I went to the same public high school in Michigan as Adam Herz, the screenwriter of *American Pie*, where I was first chair of the tuba section in the marching band.

His movie and its interminable sequels (including *American Pie: Band Camp*) made my marching band the punchline of a national joke. Although it's been almost thirty years since I've sat in the bleachers of a high school football game playing music for a team and community that belittled me and my friends, the sting never quite goes away.

I wrote this play to give my younger self the sense of agency it never had and in so doing hopefully it gives you a sense of agency now.

NOTE ON MUSIC

Regarding stage directions where music is heard or characters are directed to sing, license to produce *BLEACHERS* does not include a performance license for any third-party or copyrighted music. Licensees should create an original composition or use music in the public domain. For further information, please see the Music and Third-Party Materials Use Note on page iii.

NOTES FOR THE DIRECTOR

Monologues

There is a symbiotic relationship between the band, the announcer, the referee's whistle, and the game itself. The band is required to fill up any lag time in the game with high-spirited music – i.e., during timeouts, moving the chains for a new set of downs, etc. – but since the interval of down time is usually quite short, the band only plays a few measures of music. They never play music while the football team is actually engaged in the game. The snippets of songs exist to fire up the crowd but never to distract the football players from the game. But the tuba section never plays the fight song, they play themselves, speaking their hearts in place of music.

Chorus/Floating Ensemble

BLEACHERS is designed to scale. While the central story can be told with just the four actors playing the tuba section, the presence of a Chorus can be drawn from other members of the marching band, kids in the theater department, or any other students from the broader reality of high school that are overlooked, half heard, or nearly forgotten. In the appendix you'll find a number of brief Choral interludes. Use all of them. Choose a few. Invent your own in your rhythm. Use them as a visual echo, or a musical underscore, or as a reminder that the four tuba players in the bleachers are never really alone. Encourage your students to contribute ideas for Chorus moments. Give them agency. Let them rewrite silence.

Localization

BLEACHERS is also designed to be hyper-local. The more personal it feels to your school and community, the more powerful it becomes. You are encouraged to: swap in your school mascot and colors, reference your actual fight song, use local place names, "Behind the Casey's" or "Over by the east gym," and let students insert inside jokes or custom chants where appropriate. Feel free to modify background details, school-specific terminology, and any line that would make students say, "That's not how we talk."

This is a script built to adapt. The goal is recognition.

Let the audience see themselves. Let the students tell their vision.

Make it yours. Make it true. Make it LOUD.

For everyone in high school who feels like they're in the background of someone else's story

(That's seventeen-year-old me carrying the sousaphone.)

The Season Opener

(Friday night.)

(A high school football stadium.)

(The bleachers.)

(More accurately, the back of the bleachers.)

(The tuba section is always in the back of every place they inhabit, the music room, the bus, the bleachers, it doesn't matter. They are invisible to everyone and thus able to watch everyone else, the rest of the band, the student section, and of course the football field, too.)

NEIL. Do you think tubas remember their players?

ELIZA. The quarterback's neck is thicker than my torso.

JOY. Anybody with two first names makes me suspicious.

NEIL. Like, when after I graduate, will the next person have to earn my tuba's trust again?

ELIZA. What are you babbling about, Neil?

NEIL. Memory.

Loss.

Continuance.

JOY. Your tuba won't remember you.

No one will remember any of us.

We're the background noise of the real story.

ELIZA. We're not the background, we're the underscore.

JOY. Down on that field are the kids who will be remembered.

The marching band?

We're the help.

ANNOUNCER. Touchdown, East Grand Rapids!!

#24, Thrillin' Dylan Anderson!!!!

(The crowd goes wild.)

(The members of the tuba section do not.)

(They strap on their extremely cumbersome tubas and stand to play the fight song.)

ELIZA. "Once more, into the breach, dear friends."

NEIL. "Unto the breach."

ELIZA. Unto?

NEIL. "Do unto others as you would have them do unto you."

ELIZA. Unto.

You're sure?

NEIL. *Henry V*, Act Three, Scene One.

When I was twelve my Dad made me memorize inspiring speeches to counteract slothfulness.

I'm sure.

ELIZA. "Once more, unto the breach, dear friends."

ANNOUNCER. The East Grand Rapids Marching Band invites you to sing along to the fight song, "Onward East High"!

*(**JOY** is section leader.)*

JOY. Let's put a little extra juice on the fight song, people.

> *(Four whistles from the unseen drum major, Kate.)*

Rusty, follow me.

> *(Lights shift.)*

> *(Instead of playing the fight song* **RUSTY** *speaks to the audience [which is the central conceit of* Bleachers, *at every impetus to play music, the tuba players reveal their inner lives instead].)*

RUSTY. *(To us.)* I don't want to be here.

Not like, existentially.

Here-here.

In these bleachers.

In my fourteen-year-old skin.

Everyone always acts like I'm fine.

Because I show up.

But showing up isn't the same as being okay.

I feel like I'm holding up a mirror that's reflecting everyone else and nothing of me.

Do you know that feeling?

Like, when you become a really good version of, "Don't worry, I'm fine."

I want to go home.

But I don't know where home is anymore.

> *(Lights shift.)*

> *(The fight song just ended.* **RUSTY** *didn't do so well.)*

ELIZA. What does it feel like to be a musical prodigy?

RUSTY. I am so sorry.

NEIL. Probably akin to Mozart resting his fingers on the piano keys for the first time

JOY. Don't listen to them.

ELIZA. They didn't have pianos back then only harpsichords.

NEIL. Probably akin to Mozart resting his fingers on the harpsichord keys for the first time.

ELIZA. What I wouldn't give to be touched by the gods like you have been, freshman.

RUSTY. I don't mean to be a burden.

JOY. You're not a burden, Rusty, you're new, and everybody knows what it feels like to have to start at the beginning.

Right?

ELIZA. We're supposed to make him feel better right now?

He just made all our lives harder.

Especially yours, Joy.

ANNOUNCER. Caledonia to kick off from their own 25-yard line.

> *(A tradition: everyone stomps the bleachers, holds their hands above their heads, wiggles their fingers and says, "Aaaaaaaaaaaahhhh" until the ball is kicked; then they drop their hands, and the* **BAND MEMBERS**, *except* **RUSTY** *[because no one told him], all say:)*

ELIZA, NEIL & JOY. Crescendo!!

ELIZA. As far as I can recollect, freshman, you're the only band member who signed up at the beginning of the semester.

NEIL. Thus missing the glories of band camp.

RUSTY. It was a last minute decision.

I'm really grateful to Mr. Papalko for letting me join so late.

ELIZA. Why the change of heart?

RUSTY. My parents wanted me to play in the band.

ELIZA. Music lovers, are they?

RUSTY. No.

It's so I can appear well-rounded on my college applications.

NEIL. You signed up to play the tuba to get into college?!?

The price is too high, sir.

RUSTY. I signed up for band to get into college, Mr. Papalko sent me to you because I can't even read music.

NEIL. Mr. Papalko always makes the rejects play the tuba.

ELIZA. He made you play the tuba, too.

NEIL. Need I say more?

JOY. Not being able to read music raises the difficulty of my job by a few orders of ten, Rusty.

RUSTY. If it's easier I can just pretend to play.

JOY. It's definitely easier but it's also unacceptable.

As section leader I'm responsible for your musical and marching abilities.

You pretending to play would be a failure of leadership on my part.

RUSTY. Maybe I could switch to another instrument?

ELIZA. You got sent to the seventh circle of hell, freshman, it's a one-way ticket.

NEIL. Back of the bleachers.

The farthest you can get from social acceptance.

RUSTY. Playing the tuba can't be that bad.

NEIL. Ummmmmmm.

ANNOUNCER. Interception, East Grand Rapids!!

#10, Mike Edison!!

(The crowd goes wild.)

(The tuba players do not.)

(Lights shift. **ELIZA** *speaks to the audience.)*

ELIZA. *(To us.)* I used to pretend I was invisible.

Not metaphorically, literally invisible.

I'd walk the halls like I was the hero of a stealth video game.

Avoid eye contact.

Step-light.

Slouch.

Hide.

Because if I was invisible, then it made sense that nobody saw me.

But being invisible isn't safe, it's lonely.

I don't need to be the main character.

I just want to be noticed enough to be in the credits.

"Tuba Player #3," I'm not even asking to have a name.

Maybe someday soon someone will notice me enough that I can feel real.

(Lights shift.)

JOY. You signed up for social self-immolation, Rusty.

NEIL. The berets!

JOY. We don't even get regular band helmets.

Which look stupid enough, but what pimply teenager can rock a beret?

NEIL. I come close.

ELIZA. You come nowhere near close, Neil.

None of us do.

The tuba section are an island unto ourselves.

NEIL. The outcasts of outcasts.

ELIZA. If the marching band is the lowest social caste in high school, tuba players are the Untouchables.

RUSTY. There's not an egalitarian sense of shame among all band members?

ELIZA. Oh, Lord no.

JOY. Each instrument has its own character and they unilaterally think they're better than us.

ELIZA. Up front are the flutes.

Almost all girls who act superior because they get the most melodies.

JOY. Trumpets are mostly young men with a lot to prove.

NEIL. I was a trumpet player until I realized ambition is societal conditioning.

ELIZA. And because your embouchure is too weak to get close to the high notes.

NEIL. You really know how to hurt a guy.

JOY. Clarinets are a good mixture of musicianship and humility but still manage to stick up their noses at us.

ELIZA. Saxophones are groovy but some think they're a latter-day John Coltrane.

JOY. French horns have the same mouthpiece as the trumpet and are for the kids not good enough to play the trumpet.

NEIL. The French horn was my final unsuccessful attempt to not be made a tuba player.

ELIZA. Trombones and baritones aren't cool at all but a little bit cooler than we are thus they also get to look down on us.

NEIL. And then there's an empty row so that people can walk from one side of the band room to the other without having to get too close to the smelly cubbyholes for people's shoes.

JOY. And then there's us.

ELIZA. We are the worst musicians playing the easiest parts.

NEIL. Least gifted.

ELIZA. Excuse me, least gifted musicians and the scourge of all of high school.

RUSTY. If it's so bad why did you choose to be in band in the first place?

NEIL. Are you speaking to me?

RUSTY. I'm speaking to all of you.

NEIL. Then I will answer for myself.

I joined band because I worship music and want to know everything about it but attend a public school in the United States of America.

ELIZA. The only reason the music program can exist is because we are a functionary to the football team.

Arts funding?

Who cares?

No, let's worship the fate of a stupidly shaped ball instead.

ANNOUNCER. Touchdown, East Grand Rapids!!

#24, Thrillin' Dylan Anderson!!!!

(The crowd goes wild.)

(Lights shift. **NEIL** *speaks to the audience.)*

NEIL. *(To us.)* I think failure is a form of time travel.

Like, when you mess up bad enough, your brain launches you twenty minutes, twenty days, twenty years in the future to when you're lying in bed thinking about this exact moment and whispering, "Why did I do that?"

And in the meantime, like the present moment, just kind of evaporates.

You don't get to live it.

Which sucks, because I think life is mostly made of mistakes.

And if we time travel through all of them, what's left?

(Lights shift.)

JOY. We're all here in part because we love music.

NEIL. Worship music.

ELIZA. Need music.

JOY. What kind of music do you listen to, Rusty?

RUSTY. I don't?

JOY. Ummmm.

NEIL. Oh, wow.

ELIZA. Hopeless.

JOY. You don't listen to music?

RUSTY. I mean, when it's on in the car.

Or in waiting rooms.

NEIL. Do you even like music?

RUSTY. I like it, but I guess it doesn't speak to me the way it speaks to some people?

Like it's a transmission on the radio but I don't get the signal.

ELIZA. The love of music is the only thing we all have in common.

RUSTY. Then I guess we won't be friends.

ELIZA. That's the thing, we're not friends.

NEIL. Friend-ly.

JOY. Respectful.

NEIL. Co-workers.

ELIZA. Where do you live, Joy?

JOY. 1842 Sherman.

ELIZA. Huh.

JOY. You?

ELIZA. 232 San Luis Rey.

JOY. By the grocery store?

ELIZA. No, the other side.

JOY. Oh. Nice.

ELIZA. Neil, where do you live?

NEIL. You don't really care.

ELIZA. I don't really care because we know each other in the bleachers and that's it.

Neil, what grade are you in?

NEIL. Senior.

You?

ELIZA. Sophomore.

NEIL. Joy?

JOY. Junior.

ELIZA. We don't have any of the same classes because we're all in different grades.

NEIL. Except Joy and I have Physics third period.

JOY. Did you look at this week's problem set?

NEIL. I finished it already.

JOY. Since this morning?

NEIL. The answers appeared on the back of my eyelids as I slept through gym.

JOY. Because I'm completely lost.

NEIL. I can help reveal the open secret order of the universe if it would be useful.

JOY. That would be fantastic, Neil, I feel like I'm drowning.

RUSTY. How do you sleep through gym?

ELIZA. Hush!

Outside of band class, Physics, and the bleachers, we don't know each other.

RUSTY. I get it.

You're not friends you're bound instead by a common suffering, enduring physical hardships and mockery from our community and playing the tuba will define my entire existence.

ELIZA. We're only offering the truth, freshman.

RUSTY. My name's Rusty.

ELIZA. I know what your name is, I choose to call you freshman out of disdain.

JOY. It's still the first two weeks of the semester.

JOY. You can add/drop classes without penalty, as section leader I'd have to sign a form but I'll sign it no problem and maybe save us all a lot of unnecessary suffering.

ELIZA. Save yourself.

NEIL. Save the integrity of your back from forty pounds of pure hell digging into your shoulders for four quarters.

> (**NEIL** *indicates the towels that he and the others have wrapped around their instruments and secured with tape to protect their shoulders.*)

RUSTY. If my presence here offends you, I'm sorry.

I'll do my best to become proficient as a tuba player but I'm not going to quit.

ANNOUNCER. Time-out, East Grand Rapids.

JOY. Remember to watch drum major Kate's signals for the fills.

We stand and flip to the page of whatever number fingers she holds up.

How many fingers is she holding up?

RUSTY. Four.

ELIZA. Congratulations, freshman.

That's the first thing you've done right in your high school marching band career.

> (*The tubas flip to page four.*)

JOY. What song will we be playing, Rusty?

RUSTY. "The Imperial March" from *Star Wars*.

NEIL. Or in layman's nomenclature, "The Darth Vader Theme."

JOY. Lucky for you, it's one of the easiest tuba parts in the world.

> *(**JOY** calls out the notes as **ELIZA** and **NEIL** hum along.)*

G, G, G, E, G, E.

G, G, G, E, E, E, G, G, G, G.

You play with the index, middle, and ring fingers only.

Let's label them one, two, and three in that order, and when I say zero that means none of your fingers touch the keys.

> *(Four whistles from drum major Kate.)*

I'll call out the fingering as we go.

Ready?

RUSTY. No.

> *(Lights shift. **JOY** speaks to the audience.)*

JOY. *(To us.)* I hate the word extracurricular.

Like what we do doesn't count.

Like this, playing music, this thing that saves me a little bit every day is just extra.

Extra noise.

Extra cost.

We're not extra. We're essential.

The bleachers are the only place I feel like I belong without having to explain why.

> *(Lights shift.)*

ELIZA. I saw a video of a band kid in Arkansas playing his French horn alone on the sideline while the football team huddled, completely oblivious to him even though he was playing music six feet in front of them. And I thought it was the saddest thing I'd ever seen.

JOY. You see?

> To them we'll always be nothing but background noise.
> They think we exist to make their story more epic.

ELIZA. But maybe that is the story.

JOY. What?

ELIZA. To be the kid who played anyway.

JOY. No matter if anyone is listening or not.

ELIZA. Not the underscore. The scaffolding.

> Invisible but without it everything falls apart.

> *(The tuba section watches the football continue
> as the lights fade.)*

The Injury

(The following Friday night.)

(A high school football stadium.)

(The bleachers.)

*(**RUSTY** now has a towel wrapped around his sousaphone and secured with tape to keep it from digging into his shoulder.)*

*(**ELIZA** and **NEIL** are watching the game.)*

*(**JOY** and **RUSTY** are both holding their mouthpieces and looking at sheet music.)*

NEIL. Who referees high school football games?

Are they in a union?

ELIZA. One fifty a game, cash.

NEIL. Is that reportable income?

My cousin who's a waitress went to jail for not reporting her tips.

And I was like, doesn't the American justice system have bigger problems?

She's not even that good a waitress, it's not like she was bringing in tens of thousands of dollars.

*(**JOY** plays a tone into her mouthpiece.)*

JOY. Match that tone, Rusty.

*(**RUSTY** tries.)*

Tighten your lips.

Tighter.

> (**JOY** *plays the tone again.*)

> (**RUSTY** *is able to match it.*)

> (*And then she plays a very low note.*)

> (**RUSTY** *is able to match that, too.*)

JOY. Now connect the two using six notes in between.

> (**JOY** *starts on the low note and plays a scale.*)

> (**RUSTY** *does the same.*)

Now let's try to put it together on the instrument.

> (**RUSTY** *puts his mouthpiece into his tuba.*)

I'll call out the notes, you say the fingering and then play it.

> (**NEIL** *and* **ELIZA** *continue to watch the game.*)

ELIZA. What if we used the metric system?

Would football still exist?

NEIL. Liberia, Myanmar, and us.

The only three countries who still use the imperial system as their standard unit of measurement.

JOY. B-flat.

RUSTY. One three.

> (*He plays the note on the tuba correctly [and does so for all the following notes, too].*)

JOY. C.

RUSTY. One two.

JOY. D.

RUSTY. Two.

JOY. E-flat.

RUSTY. Zero.

JOY. F.

RUSTY. One three.

JOY. G.

RUSTY. One two.

JOY. A.

RUSTY. Two.

JOY. B-flat.

RUSTY. Zero.

JOY. Now put it all together.

(**RUSTY** *plays the B-flat scale.*)

Congratulations, Rusty.

You just played your first scale.

RUSTY. I've got a good teacher.

ELIZA. Don't get ahead of yourself, freshman, Miles Davis isn't looking over his shoulder quite yet.

JOY. But it's a beginning.

ELIZA. Yes.

It's a –

(*A nasty injury happens on the field.*)

(*A football player screams like a wild animal howling in pain.*)

(*The air of the entire stadium is sucked out.*)

RUSTY. Oh my god.

NEIL. I think I saw his femur go through his leg.

ELIZA. It was his tibia.

NEIL. No, the tibia is on the lower leg, that's definitely his upper leg.

JOY. I'm going to be sick.

> (**JOY** *runs off quickly.*)

> (*A* **MOTHER** *in the crowd realizes it's her son that is injured.*)

MOTHER. Scott!!!!!!!!!!!!!!!!!!!!!!!!!!!!!!!!!!

> (*Woah, that's intense.*)

> (*Thousands of silent people is scary.*)

ANNOUNCER. Injury time-out.

> (*It's silent.*)

> (*It continues to be silent.*)

> (*It's really bad.*)

> (*They have to bring out the ambulance.*)

> (*Lights shift.* **ELIZA** *speaks to the audience.*)

ELIZA. (*To us.*) I think I understand football now.
Not the rules, the theology.
It's about punishment.
About proving how much pain you can take before you get to celebrate.
And it's beautiful in that way that makes you feel sick.
The crowd, the players, they believe this matters.
Last week I felt a pulse.
Like I was part of the story, even if no one noticed I was in the frame.

It was.

Unfamiliar.

I'm so used to being in the negative space around someone else's spotlight.

But maybe I'm not just the background.

Maybe I'm becoming a whole background.

> *(Lights turn to normal.)*

Look at that young man, his tibia sticking straight through his leg.

NEIL. His femur.

ELIZA. His femur.

That young man might never walk again and I guarantee you there are twenty boys on that sideline hoping they'll be the ones to take his spot.

NEIL. Sure, starters all get their own Booster Girl.

RUSTY. The girls in skimpy clothes who bring football players desserts?

ELIZA. And decorate their lockers and put hand-painted signs in their front yards.

NEIL. Down the street from me there are ten signs all of which read, "#32, Jeff Bird Lives Here!"

Who cares where Jeff Bird lives?

ELIZA. A Booster Girl, instant popularity, invited to the best parties, all by just taking their place in the disgusting flywheel of adolescent gladiatorial combat.

RUSTY. You're confusing their athletic achievements with their roles in the standard hierarchical system of high school.

What they do on that field might help a few of them get to college whereas without the game they would never get in.

RUSTY. And tuition free.

Good for them.

NEIL. Statistically, less than 2% of football players get college scholarships and only .23% will ever turn pro.

I don't know why I know that.

ELIZA. Because you have a photographic memory.

NEIL. Yup, that's the answer, thank you for the reminder.

ELIZA. How many clubs are you in, freshman?

RUSTY. Latin club, environmental club, and I'm running for student council.

And I'm on the newspaper and in yearbook.

And Safety Town, but that's not a club it's a volunteer activity.

ELIZA. What college admissions officer isn't going to smell lies?

RUSTY. Those are legit!

ELIZA. Weighted grades, clubs you don't care about, and volunteer activities like Safety Town?

RUSTY. Safety Town is important!

ELIZA. It's showing little kids how to cross the street.

RUSTY. Which is vital to the health of a community!

ELIZA. You live your life for another's approval, selling yourself to get out of this stupid city.

RUSTY. High school is to get somewhere else.

The facts I know now, I won't know in six months.

Do I want to participate in an educational system whose metrics are focused almost exclusively on testing?

No, but I'm in one, so I'll ace the tests.

In Boy Scouts I recently earned my basketry merit badge. I would ask, "Do you know how much I care about basketry?" but that's easy because no teenager cares about basketry.

NEIL. I do.

RUSTY. Congratulations, you're one in a billion.

NEIL. Like, deeply care.

RUSTY. Soon I'll become an Eagle Scout because to a college admissions officer who can shape the arc of my life that achievement will indicate to her the quality of person I am and my abilities as a leader.

ELIZA. You're no leader, you're a phony.

RUSTY. From the outside it won't look any different.

A disingenuous charade?

You're right.

The greatest higher educational institutions require that charade so I'll play it because I want to attain a better life.

ELIZA. Joy is a leader, not you.

She could have asked you not to play.

That's what a lot of section leaders do when a new kid is too bad or too scared to play.

"Walk around with your instrument, no one will know the difference."

But because she is an actual leader she has taken it upon herself to make you proficient.

RUSTY. Joy chose to be section leader.

NEIL. She didn't.

During chair tests the only competition is to see who plays worst.

NEIL. And Joy has lost two years in a row.

To make sure I didn't become section leader during the last chair test I had Eliza hit me hard in the leg.

ELIZA. Like this.

> (**ELIZA** *hits* **NEIL** *in the leg.)*

NEIL. Owwww!

ELIZA. And because Joy is a real leader she takes her responsibility seriously.

She resents having to teach you but is too good a person to show it.

Sacrifice makes a leader.

You don't know the first thing about it.

Running for student council to appear like a leader.

I hope it works out, freshman, that you become class president.

Go to an Ivy League school.

Found a company, become a billionaire, if you're living your life in order to get something else then you might as well die now.

No matter how far you go, you can't outrun being a bitch.

NEIL. Oh, snap.

RUSTY. I'm nobody's bitch.

ELIZA. Are ya sure?

> (**NEIL** *abhors conflict and finds a way to break the ice.)*

NEIL. Did I ever tell you my dad has cancer?

ELIZA. That's hilarious, Neil.

NEIL. He has had it.

For almost eight years.

Prostate cancer.

They did a surgery, like at the beginning.

He said there was a fifty percent chance he would never get an erection again and I don't know if he got heads or tails on that coin toss because I've never asked him.

> *(Silence.)*

> *(**NEIL** definitely broke the ice.)*

> *(**ELIZA** and **RUSTY** are no longer bucking horns.)*

RUSTY. Thank you for telling us, Neil.

ELIZA. I'm so sorry your family has to go through this.

RUSTY. How are you doing?

NEIL. Most of the time the world doesn't look real and I have little faith in the meaning or purpose in our individual existence.

But other than that, it's fine.

ELIZA. If you ever want to talk about it, I'm here.

RUSTY. I'm here, too.

Not that you would ever want to talk to me because I'm a bitch.

ELIZA. You said it, not me.

NEIL. I don't want to talk about it.

I don't want to think about it.

I abhor conflict and it seemed an effective way to stop you two from fighting.

RUSTY. It worked.

ELIZA. Bravo.

RUSTY. Maybe you can work as a treaty negotiator for warring countries.

NEIL. I've often considered that myself.

> *(The injured football player is leaving the field in the ambulance.)*

ANNOUNCER. Let's give a warm East Grand Rapids salute to #12, Defensive Lineman, Scott Griffin!

> *(The crowd applauds, freaked out.)*

We appreciate your effort, Scott, and hope to see you back on the field soon!

RUSTY. Do players leave the field in an ambulance often?

ELIZA. This is my second.

NEIL. This is my fifth.

RUSTY. Fifth???

NEIL. Two spinal cord injuries, one cardiac arrest, better known as a heart attack, and Brian Dembinsky had his right leg broken so hard that when he was lying on his stomach his right foot pointed straight up to the sky.

ELIZA. There was so much blood they had to bring out the grounds crew to cover it up with lime.

The entire offensive line threw up in their hands.

NEIL. And now tonight Scott Griffin's femur bursting through his leg.

ELIZA. Look out onto that field, freshman.

Pity those young men.

Raised to believe that moving a stupidly shaped ball up and down a patch of grass will let them realize concepts they've been conditioned to desire: victory, glory, tradition, pride.

Deified now, forgotten tomorrow.

Fulfilling a fate they've never questioned.

Right in front of you is an American tragedy taking place in real time.

(A whistle.)

(The game continues.)

(It's sad how quickly the game continues.)

Hudsonville's offense looks better this year.

NEIL. The tight end is a transfer from Ottawa Hills.

(They watch a play unfold.)

ELIZA. He can catch and block.

NEIL. If our tight end last year could block like that Brian Dembinsky might still be able to walk.

ELIZA. What was the name of Belding's running back last year?

NEIL. Walter Harnancourt.

ELIZA. Harnancourt.

Gifted.

NEIL. Greasy fast.

ELIZA. Low center of gravity.

Fantastic cutback.

Remember when he broke free for that 72-yard run during conference finals?

NEIL. Leapt over our middle linebacker like a gazelle.

ELIZA. Beautiful football, like the game should be played.

(*They watch the game.*)

Uh oh.

We're bringing pressure.

Their quarterback is in trouble.

NEIL. Pump fake.

He wants to run it.

ELIZA. Scrambles.

NEIL. An off-balance throw.

ELIZA. Wobbly.

NEIL. Uh oh.

ANNOUNCER. Interception, #24, Thrillin' Dylan Anderson!

(*The* **TUBAS** *stand up to play.*)

(**JOY** *is gone, and, as second chair,* **ELIZA** *assumes the leadership position.*)

ELIZA. How many fingers is drum major Kate holding up?

RUSTY. Two.

ELIZA. Good.

Flip to, page two.

(*They all flip to page two.*)

RUSTY. Should I play or just pretend to play?

ELIZA. Play, and play loud.

RUSTY. Loud?

ELIZA. You chose to be here.

If you want to be a phony, let everybody else see you for what you are.

One, two.

One, two, three, four.

*(Lights shift. **RUSTY** speaks to the audience.)*

RUSTY. *(To us.)* It wasn't a big thing.

Before the game Joy asked, "Are you okay?"

And I said, "No."

And Joy didn't flinch.

She didn't joke it off, either.

She didn't sprint for the exit like I'd just spilled Diet Coke on her shoes.

Joy nodded.

Like it was allowed.

I've spent my life trying to make people comfortable with the version of me that can survive.

But maybe I don't want to survive.

Maybe I want to live.

To live and say weird things and cry at stupid songs and stop pretending I'm the background noise to someone else's movie.

I'm not better.

But I'm not alone, either.

And that feeling?

It's new.

(Lights shift.)

*(**ELIZA** and **NEIL** are impressed at how **RUSTY** played but don't want to say so.)*

Better?

ELIZA. Marginally.

NEIL. Barely.

ELIZA. But still terrible.

>   (**RUSTY** *can't help but smile to himself.*)

I still vote that you quit.

NEIL. I vote that you pursue your authentic self which also means I vote you quit.

ELIZA. You have one more week to add/drop classes, freshman.

The point of no return is coming.

RUSTY. I'll take it under consideration.

>   (*They watch the game.*)

ELIZA. Since when does Thrillin' Dylan play both sides of the ball?

NEIL. Coach Carmondy is trying it out this week.

ELIZA. Might be paying dividends already.

RUSTY. Who gave him the nickname Thrillin' Dylan?

NEIL. In middle school.

Pop Warner. When he was eleven.

Dylan tore off a 93-yard kickoff return and the coach said, "Thrillin' Dylan, you are my kind of football player."

RUSTY. And you know this why?

NEIL. I put a block on the far sideline during his kickoff return.

RUSTY. You played football??

ELIZA. The coach who named Thrillin' was his dad.

NEIL. If I hadn't fallen in love with music I would be down there on the field right now, much to my father's chagrin.

ELIZA. Plus marching band doesn't require drug testing.

NEIL. That sealed the deal.

RUSTY. How talented is he?

ELIZA. If Thrillin' Dylan gets the average amount of touches he's had in every other game he'll easily break the record for most career rushing yards.

NEIL. And most career touchdowns.

ELIZA. College scouts started coming when he was a sophomore.

NEIL. A five-star blue chip recruit.

ELIZA. Thrillin' Dylan is among the top ten high school running backs in the nation.

RUSTY. For people who hate the football team you know a whole lot about football.

NEIL. You will, too. If you don't quit you'll watch upwards of forty football games.

ELIZA. You'll learn the names of all the positions, players, the names of the defenses and offensive formations, no matter how hard you try not to.

RUSTY. For example.

ELIZA. For example, the offense this year is obviously based around Thrillin' Dylan, so they typically line up in a Wing-T formation, most often using the tight end as an extra blocker.

But if opponents get comfortable with the Wing-T coach has them run the single-back set on third downs over six yards.

(They call plays like a quarterback.)

NEIL. Wildcat out of the shotgun!

Bird right, 18 Premium Diesel.

ELIZA. Mao Zedong 14 left 42!

NEIL. 53 Orlando HD wide pivot F dover!

RUSTY. What do any of those mean?

ELIZA. It's a foreign language you're telling your personnel, bringing up an image for both the quarterback and the other players on offense.

The shift, the motion, the protection and then the pass routes.

It starts with one word.

Orlando.

Which is a randomly chosen word to put the play into the minds of the players.

Probably every city in the world has been used as a play call.

NEIL. Tangier on 3!

ELIZA. Hong Kong on 2!

NEIL. The suburbs of Pittsburgh on 1!

ELIZA. It could be a type of car, a bird or animal.

NEIL. Eastern Meadowlark on 2!

ELIZA. Endangered Bornean Orangutan on 4!

Or a famous person.

NEIL. Edgar Allan Poe on 1!

ELIZA. Saraswati on 2!

NEIL. Who's Saraswati?

ELIZA. The Hindu Goddess of music.

RUSTY. Can you do the full thing?

NEIL. (*As* **ANNOUNCER.**) East Grand Rapids starts the drive from their own 34-yard line.

Surprise substitution, folks, sophomore quarterback Eliza steps up to the offensive line, ready to take the snap.

ELIZA. *(As a very serious quarterback.)* FB Saraswati North Left Post 954!

> (**ELIZA** *reads the defense.*)

> *(As herself.)*

FB is to tell the fullback he's playing out of his normal position.

The 954 is a pass combination and tells three wide-receivers what to do.

4, for the outside receiver to run a square-in route.

5, for the tight end to run a seam straight up the field.

and 9, for the split end to run a skinny post.

RUSTY. What about the North Left?

ELIZA. They mean nothing, just there to make the defense think.

RUSTY. I'm impressed.

ELIZA. But I see a safety blitz from the left side, so I audible:

(As a very serious quarterback.) 16 Saraswati HD right pivot dover!

(As herself.) The additions are signals to individual players.

In our offensive play calling system, what comes after the initial random word is for the running back.

Saraswati HD.

The number before is for the offensive line.

16 Saraswati HD.

ELIZA. And finally I want a right pivot from the tight end.

So the final product becomes:

(As a very serious quarterback.) 16 Saraswati HD right pivot dover!

Hut, hut, hike!!

NEIL. *(As* **ANNOUNCER**.*)* Safety blitz.

Eliza looks left.

Looks right.

Throws.

Oh, wow, folks, a beautiful spiral so high I can barely find it in the glaring Friday night lights!

Beyond the known laws of physics the ball finds substitute wide receiver Neil in the end zone.

Touchdown, #1,992, Neil!!!!!!

> *(***NEIL*** faux cheers himself and high-fives himself, too.)*

RUSTY. I'm impressed.

ELIZA. Don't be.

I wish I wasn't able to understand the words that just came out of my mouth.

NEIL. Call a play, freshman.

(As **ANNOUNCER**.*)* The twenty-seventh string quarterback, a freshman wannabe tuba player, steps up ready to take the snap.

RUSTY. Hamlet bulldog 30 moonshot foxtrot pull trap pivot on 3!!

Hut, hut, hike!!

ELIZA. Complex offensive strategy, I'm impressed.

NEIL. *(As* **ANNOUNCER**.*)* The tuba player drops back to pass.

He scrambles.

The linebackers close in for a sack, when he pump fakes, tucks the ball and takes it himself.

The freshman tuba player breaks a tackle.

Another.

Throws a stiff arm.

RUSTY. What's a stiff arm?

ELIZA. Shhhh.

NEIL. *(As* **ANNOUNCER**.*)* The 30.

ELIZA. *(As* **ANNOUNCER**.*)* The 20.

NEIL. *(As* **ANNOUNCER**.*)* The 10.

ELIZA. *(As* **ANNOUNCER**.*)* Do you believe in miracles???

NEIL. *(As* **ANNOUNCER**.*)* Touchdown, East Grand Rapids!

> (**NEIL** *and* **ELIZA** *do faux cheering.)*

> (**RUSTY** *high-fives his* **TEAMMATES**.*)*

RUSTY. It must be amazing.

Hearing your name over the loudspeaker and the crowd cheering for you.

Even if it's only for a minute.

ELIZA. But they'll want that minute back for the rest of their lives.

They'll want to come back here, to tonight, to a moment of fame, but when we leave the bleachers, we'll always thank God we never have to come back.

> *(They watch the game.)*

ANNOUNCER. Tackle on the play, #24, Thrillin' Dylan Anderson.

NEIL. I do Thrillin' Dylan's math homework.

RUSTY. For money?

NEIL. Protection.

ELIZA. From rival Sicilian mob families?

NEIL. From him.

RUSTY. Not a great deal.

NEIL. For him it's fantastic.

RUSTY. For you.

NEIL. I don't have to worry about my physical well-being simply by carrying a few more zeroes, it's a small price to pay for peace of mind.

ELIZA. And yet we will leave this hellscape and Thrillin' Dylan will become a cop.

NEIL. Dishwasher at an all-you-can-eat buffet off the highway.

ELIZA. Assistant Manager of a fried chicken franchise.

NEIL. After high school Thrillin' Dylan will become Manager of a paper bag factory.

ELIZA. Logistics Specialist of a regional donut manufacturer.

NEIL. Investment banker.

ELIZA. Brand Manager of a gun manufacturer.

NEIL. Hazardous materials removal worker.

ELIZA. Data entry for the NSA.

NEIL. Lobbyist for big tobacco.

ELIZA. Ponzi scheme proprietor.

NEIL. Foreman of a pig slaughterhouse.

ELIZA. Weapons researcher.

NEIL. Lawyer for a pesticide company.

ELIZA. Billionaire.

NEIL. That's bad?

ELIZA. It should be illegal and morally reprehensible at the same time.

Self-interest is the common scourge that will kill our world.

RUSTY. Thrillin' Dylan will become an inground pool installer.

NEIL. There he is!

ELIZA. Strip mining company majority shareholder.

RUSTY. Billboard injury lawyer.

NEIL. 1-800-T-H-R-I-L-L-I-N'.

RUSTY. That's too many numbers.

NEIL. 1-800-T-H-R-I-L-I-N'.

ELIZA. "I outrun insurance companies that do everything in their power to not pay you even though you spend a lifetime paying obscene premiums."

NEIL. Ouch.

RUSTY. Thrillin' Dylan will become a forklift driver in a mannequin factory.

ELIZA. Oil change technician.

NEIL. Sandwich artist.

ELIZA. Lawn sprinkler crew leader.

NEIL. Line cook at a Tier II pizza restaurant.

RUSTY. Thrillin' Dylan will become a dental hygienist in a strip mall dental practice who deals prescription painkillers out of his certified pre-owned Lincoln Town Car.

*(**JOY** enters.)*

JOY. Thrillin' Dylan will become a completely average man with no passion for his job or family, a man who harbors a gnawing sense of dissatisfaction, a quiet rage at the injustice that his best days are long behind him and he's seen as simply another normal person because he knows the cheers and admiration he knew in his youth are the correct measure of his worth and that this silent life he lives now is the lie.

NEIL. Totally.

ELIZA. That's him.

JOY. I just watched Scott Griffin leave the stadium grounds in an ambulance.

His mother wailing, his father was numb.

Scott's entire life just changed forever.

ELIZA. A gift.

JOY. A gift?

ELIZA. That young man had to in one moment reckon with all his choices leading to this moment and now has to imagine a different future.

Who is he now?

Take the uniform off, the shoulder pads, and what's left?

Traumatic now, okay, I don't envy his journey and I don't wish him physical pain, but Scott Griffin has been given the great gift of being forced to discover who he truly is.

(Slight pause.)

JOY. If I tell you a secret do you swear to never repeat it ever again?

ELIZA. Not even under torture.

NEIL. We're probably the ideal people to tell a secret because we don't know any of the same people.

JOY. Rusty?

RUSTY. I'm honored you would tell any secret to me, Joy, I would never betray that trust.

ELIZA. She's not telling it to you, freshman, you just happen to be here.

RUSTY. I can throw myself off the top of the bleachers if you'd feel more comfortable.

JOY. No, I trust you.

(Wow.)

(In that moment **JOY** *realizes she does in fact trust* **RUSTY**, *a fact lost on none of them, least of all* **RUSTY**.*)*

Last summer my cousin invited me to this three-day music festival where everybody camps out and doesn't shower and pees in porta potties.

Normally I would have said no.

Every time I look into the standing lake of poopy water I imagine a snake pulling me down into the muck and drowning me in other people's fecal matter, urine, and used tampons.

NEIL. Happened to a friend of an acquaintance of mine.

JOY. But I made a commitment to myself when I turned sixteen to do something that challenges my sensibilities once a month because suffering is the necessary price of growth so I said yes.

The music at the festival was awful and I am not one of those people who "dances like nobody's watching" no matter how much I wish I was.

JOY. I told my cousin I wasn't feeling well and was going back to the tent to rest.

She was so gone she didn't even ask if I wanted a ride. The walk back to the campground was four miles. My feet were killing me and I was starving.

NEIL. Oh, no.

JOY. But then I saw a huge gas station that seemed to light up the entire sky.

NEIL. Oh, wow.

JOY. I strolled the aisles, picking out an assortment of candy and trashy snacks.

Behind the window of the cash register was a giant luna moth.

I was struck dumb it was so beautiful.

And the cashier, a girl not much older than me said, "Did you know a luna moth's only function is to be beautiful, to pass on life, and to die? Last year during a period of emotional crisis I prayed for help and a luna moth was sent to let me see a proof of God."

The cashier's name tag read Sadie, there was a light behind her eyes when she smiled and for the first time in my life I knew for sure who I was.

I wanted to blurt out "your smile let me know I'm queer" but left without saying a word. Back at camp I ate every piece of candy and empty calorie I could find; my cousin threw up coconut rum most of the night and I had to hold her hair.

We went home the next morning and I've never told anyone about Sadie or how I think about her smile at least a thousand times a day.

ELIZA. Thank you for trusting us enough to share your story.

RUSTY. I'm honored you told us, Joy.

ELIZA. Are you going to come out to your family?

JOY. We're Traditionalist Catholics who don't recognize the reforms of the Second Vatican Council.

NEIL. Sounds like that's a no.

JOY. Homosexuality is a mortal sin.

Last week at dinner I obliquely asked, "What if a friend of a friend of a friend of mine happened to think they might be potentially but probably not gay."

NEIL. How did it go?

JOY. My father said that they would burn in hell for eternity and that their family should be shamed for having failed in their duties.

RUSTY. But that situation was theoretical.

You're their daughter.

ELIZA. It's like when some hardcore right wing politician proclaims "no abortions even for rape" but his own daughter gets raped by a group of prison convicts and he's like, "psych, just kidding."

JOY. No. It's real, and every day I wake up with this terrible secret.

I smile at meals, I kiss them goodbye when I go to school but I know that if I say the words, "I'm queer" they'll turn their backs on me.

ELIZA. How long have you known?

JOY. I think part of me has always known. But that night at a gas station in the middle of nowhere I found out for sure.

NEIL. Three years you've been holding onto this?

JOY. I graduate in two years, and I think maybe I can get out of the house without them knowing.

ELIZA. But you have to tell them.

JOY. I don't.

ELIZA. It's who you are!

No matter what happens we'll be here for you.

(Pause.)

JOY. Hey, do you guys want to do something after the game tonight?

NEIL. I have just cleared my schedule.

JOY. Eliza?

What do you think?

ELIZA. I think it's about time we saw each other out of the office.

JOY. Then it's settled.

NEIL. What about him?

RUSTY. Me?

I don't have ears, don't worry about it.

JOY. Rusty, would you like to join us?

RUSTY. No, thank you.

JOY. Tonight will be the first time the tuba section will spend time together not in the band room or the bleachers.

It would be very meaningful if all of us could be together as a complete section.

RUSTY. I appreciate your charade, Joy, but I've got to work on my Landscape Architecture merit badge.

NEIL. Not to mention your presidential campaign.

ELIZA. Kissing babies, pressing the flesh.

JOY. You'll be missed, Rusty.

RUSTY. I'm not sure that's true.

NEIL. Now we know the personnel, but what are we going to do?

ELIZA. We could go to Denny's.

They have two-for-one breakfast after eleven p.m.

NEIL. My cousin's a waitress there.

JOY. The one who went to jail for unreported tips?

NEIL. Early parole.

She says never go to Denny's, it's completely unsanitary, like pubic hair and spider eggs unsanitary.

JOY & ELIZA. Ewwwwwww!!!

JOY. We could go to the field behind the apple orchard and look at the stars.

ELIZA. Or we could drive around aimlessly and sing along to music.

JOY. That sounds perfect.

NEIL. Look out, y'all, I have in my possession a serious set of pipes.

(**NEIL** *sings with great confidence.*)

(*Regardless of whether the actor playing* **NEIL** *has serious pipes or not, he sings with great confidence.*)

JOY. Are you sure you don't want to come, Rusty?

RUSTY. I hope you all have a great time.

(*They're so happy he's not coming but don't want him to know.*)

(**RUSTY** *knows, and feels incredibly alone.*)

Homecoming

(A couple Friday nights later.)

(A high school football stadium.)

(The bleachers.)

ANNOUNCER. And now, introducing this year's homecoming court!

Paige Adloff and Alan Heffron!

NEIL. Watch this, Rusty, every couple in the homecoming court rides in golf carts around the football field waving like they just came back from the moon.

> (**NEIL** *and* **JOY** *pretend they're riding in a golf cart and wave like they just got back from the moon.)*

"What was your favorite aspect of our moon landing, Science Officer Joy?"

JOY. "That would have to be keeping my mind on all my loved ones back on earth wishing I'd come home safely. How about you, Chief Petty Officer Neil?"

NEIL. Chief Petty Officer?

JOY. Co-Pilot?

NEIL. Not Mission Commander?

JOY. You're not exactly leadership material, Neil, I'm not saying anything new here.

NEIL. Can we at least pretend?

"Fake it till you make it," right?

RUSTY. Anybody going to the homecoming dance tomorrow night?

NEIL. Nope.

JOY. Me, neither.

ELIZA. We've got relatives from out of town coming to stay with us.

You?

RUSTY. Dances aren't really my thing.

ELIZA. What is your thing, freshman?

NEIL. Brown nosing.

ELIZA. Doing things for promise of a return not for their inherence.

NEIL. Thinking you're superior to other people because they don't share your unoriginal life goals.

RUSTY. It's so gratifying to be seen.

ELIZA. The freshman understands sarcasm, it's a miracle!

ANNOUNCER. Brooke Sobota and Dylan Anderson!

ELIZA. 100:1 on Thrillin' Dylan being Homecoming King.

NEIL. That's an absurd risk.

Those odds only make sense at scale.

If I bet one dollar and Alan Heffron is homecoming king you owe me a hundred.

ELIZA. Then you have nothing to lose.

NEIL. I'm in.

One dollar.

JOY. I'm in, too.

Five dollars.

ELIZA. Freshman?

You want in on the action?

RUSTY. No, thanks, but I did want to ask you, Neil, is the limo coming tomorrow to pick you up at six-thirty or six, I forget.

NEIL. Six p.m. sharp.

ELIZA. Shhhhhh.

JOY. Limo?

What limo?

ELIZA. Who talked?

NEIL. I talk in my sleep so if Rusty broke into my house and stood by my bed all night I may have said something.

RUSTY. Nobody talked.

Our phone number is one digit off a limo company, and every year during homecoming and prom we always get a few calls of kids trying to reserve a limo for a dance.

Last spring during prom I was in an off mood and totally booked a limo ride for some poor kid.

Probably screwed his entire prom experience.

ANNOUNCER. Wendy Wright and Jeff Bird!

NEIL. Wait, I reserved a limo last prom and it never showed up.

RUSTY. Whoops.

NEIL. You asshole.[*]

Helene Turner and I were probably going to get married.

(**NEIL** *lunges at* **RUSTY**, *gives him a stiff arm.*)

ELIZA. That's a stiff arm.

RUSTY. Section leader, help!

(**JOY** *separates them.*)

---

[*] Alternatively: **NEIL**. You rogue!

JOY. All right, boys, break it up!

ELIZA. You went to the prom with Helene Turner?

NEIL. No, because she accused me of lying about the limo so she went with Mike Rosander and I stayed home and cried.

ELIZA. But you were supposed to.

JOY. She's like Ms. East Grand Rapids, how did you pull that off?

NEIL. I did her math homework since fourth grade, she owed me.

ANNOUNCER. Melissa Coolidge and Paul Mead!

JOY. I've never been to a dance.

NEIL. Me neither, thanks to this asshole.*

ELIZA. Last year I went to the Valentine's Dance ironically.

NEIL. How do you go to a dance ironically?

ELIZA. I brought my thirty-two-year-old cousin as my date and wore a dress I made from paper plates.

NEIL. You are my hero.

ANNOUNCER. Rebecca Jackson and A.J. Graham!

RUSTY. It was you who I spoke to on the phone, was it not, Joy?

You were inquiring about a limo with a disco light inside.

JOY. Okay, yes, we are going to the dance together, Rusty, would you like to come with us?

I apologize for not asking you sooner.

NEIL. It was your idea!

---

*Alternatively: **NEIL**. Me neither, thanks to this lowlife.

JOY. Which I have felt terrible about since I had it.

ELIZA. We don't want you to come but will you come so Joy can stop feeling guilty?

RUSTY. No, thanks, I have to prepare for my first meeting as freshman class president.

NEIL. Congratulations on the stunning victory.

ELIZA. Have you already received the key to the nuclear codes, Mr. President?

NEIL. How many agents are in your Secret Service detail?

RUSTY. You're being hilarious.

NEIL. I especially connected to your "healthy hot lunch" campaign.

ELIZA. But your coup de grâce was the call for a portable library for the cafeteria.

"Reading And Eating."

Did you come up with that policy name yourself or did you delegate it to your Chief of Staff?

RUSTY. I remain laughing on the inside.

JOY. Okay, let's give Mr. President a break.

Congratulations, though, Rusty, we're all proud of your victory.

RUSTY. I feel lucky to be able to represent my class and will fulfill the duties of my office to my utmost abilities.

NEIL. So you can sell yourself to get into college.

RUSTY. I want a future that's not here.

I'll learn to spin plates on my nose if necessary.

ELIZA. Speaking of your future, I got a call from an army recruitment officer a couple weeks ago, he asked me about my plans after high school, I said I was a card-carrying communist.

NEIL. You have a card?

ELIZA. After agreeing that the armed forces probably weren't a right fit he asked if I knew of anyone who's serious about college who is well-rounded and of course I mentioned you.

RUSTY. What??

ELIZA. You should expect a visit to your home by Sergeant Renner.

RUSTY. The military is like the last thing I ever want to do with my life.

ELIZA. You're already a Boy Scout.

RUSTY. That's for show!

I don't want to become some zombie jarhead.

JOY. Shut your mouth!

> *(Woah.)*

> *(**JOY** doesn't raise her voice very much but it's scary when she does.)*

You want to know why we chose to play the tuba, Rusty.

I did it for my family.

In high school my dad was the drum major and my mom was the first chair of the trumpet section.

My family believes in tradition and duty.

My father served in the military, my grandfather, too.

What do you know about service, Rusty?

It might be convenient to be above everything and not have to connect to anything of substance outside your own personal gain.

Military personnel believe in honor, loyalty and service.

JOY. You call those whatever words you want.

But they are noble, and they take sacrifice.

RUSTY. I'm sorry, Joy.

JOY. Don't apologize to me.

I'm sorry for you, Rusty.

I want to protect you.

You chose to be here, whatever your motivations and you haven't quit yet, which I admire, especially since your fellow section members haven't made your time here very comfortable.

ELIZA. *(To* **NEIL**.*)* She's looking at you.

NEIL. She's looking at you more!

JOY. I'll do my best to make you proficient at marching and music because that's my duty as your section leader but I will not allow you to denigrate what I believe to be a noble pursuit.

        (**RUSTY** *begins to silently weep.*)

I'm sorry to make you silently weep, Rusty, but honesty is showing respect for another person.

RUSTY. Jeff Bird beat me up yesterday.

JOY. What?

Why didn't you say something?

RUSTY. Because you guys think I'm a brown-nosing phony!

ELIZA. Because that's true!

JOY. That's enough, Eliza!

ELIZA. You told me you resent having to teach him if he's here to get a gold star.

JOY. Which was said in confidence.

RUSTY. Is that true?

JOY. Yes, it is.

Your presence makes my job more difficult, Rusty, and I have a lot going on in my life.

But it's unbecoming of a section leader to gossip about my subordinates and for that I apologize.

ELIZA. Brown-nosing phony or not, you don't deserve to get beat up.

NEIL. Not by Jeff Bird, anyway.

ELIZA. Right.

If you're going to get beat up at least get beat up by a real badass.

NEIL. You got beat up by like a Tier II bully, which is kind of more sad than anything else.

RUSTY. I didn't hear the apology, but I appreciate the sentiment.

ANNOUNCER. And now the moment you've been waiting for.

This year's Homecoming King is, you guessed it, Thrillin' Dylan Anderson!

Accompanied by his Queen, Brooke Sobota!!!!

ELIZA. You owe me one dollar and you owe me five.

NEIL. I'm not very liquid at the moment, you'll have to float me.

ANNOUNCER. Please join the band as they celebrate with Bon Jovi's "It's My Life"!

(Lights shift.)

*(***ELIZA*** and ***NEIL*** *speak to the audience but don't hear each other.)*

NEIL. *(To us.)* Eliza says the weirdest things.

Like the other day she said, "Do you think stars ever get tired of being wished on?"

And I was like, what kind of brain just pulls that out after playing the fight song?

ELIZA. *(To us.)* Neil says the weirdest things.

Last week he said, "Time is like teeth, it only hurts when you notice it."

What???

NEIL. *(To us.)* She always sits like she's hiding something under her posture.

Like, if she uncrossed her arms, the sky might fall in.

People don't talk to her much.

Which is wild, because she's got this quiet that feels earned.

ELIZA. *(To us.)* He doesn't care how people see him.

Or if he does, he's made peace with the part of himself that never performs.

Which is insane.

And kind of holy.

NEIL. *(To us.)* Sometimes I catch her watching the field.

Like she's decoding it, not a game but a riddle, and she's two steps away from solving it forever.

And when Eliza laughs, not politely, but actually laughs, it sounds like someone let a secret slip.

ELIZA. *(To us.)* If he ever said, "Come with me," I would follow him.

I don't know where we'd go.

But I think the silence would be kind there.

(Lights back to normal.)

(Neither are aware of what truly lies in the other's heart.)

JOY. What happened with Jeff Bird, Rusty?

RUSTY. I don't like to waste time to go to my locker between classes so I carry all my books for the day in my backpack.

NEIL. We've noticed.

ELIZA. You walk the halls like Tenzing Norgay summiting Everest in 1953.

RUSTY. With all those books my center of gravity is off, and as I passed the senior lockers on my way to Latin class Jeff Bird grabbed the straps of my backpack and pulled my legs out from underneath me.

NEIL. Chad Venturi, now that's a Tier I bully.

ELIZA. You wouldn't have a spleen if Chad Venturi was giving you the business.

RUSTY. Just asked me if I'd forgotten the combination to my locker.

"No."

"Then what is it?"

"45-12-32."

ELIZA. The nuclear codes!!

JOY. Shhhhh.

RUSTY. Jeff said, "So use your locker instead. You already look like an asshole[*] carrying the tuba, give yourself a few hours a day to look normal."

So now I waste half my time putting my books in my locker because I don't want to get my legs taken out from underneath me.

---

[*] Alternatively: **RUSTY**. … You already look like an idiot carrying the tuba…

JOY. Rusty, I'm sorry you had to go through that.

ELIZA. Congratulations, you popped your cherry!

RUSTY. But the school says they have zero tolerance for bullying.

NEIL. Good-intentioned lies.

JOY. They have the power to laugh at all the kids in the marching band without censure.

ELIZA. Football players' behavior is tacitly sanctioned by a system that celebrates sports and not the arts.

NEIL. They get to humiliate us.

ELIZA. Make us a punchline.

"This one time, at band camp..."

RUSTY. I'm not familiar.

NEIL. A running joke in the entire school is that band members are so boring that we begin every story with, "This one time, at band camp..."

RUSTY. Hilarious.

ELIZA. It gets even funnier after you've heard it for the thousandth time.

JOY. This one time at band camp we worked our asses off through sweaty hot August days at a run-down YMCA camp to learn how to entertain you so shut your mouth about what we did at band camp.

NEIL. Eliza, what was your first experience with shame at the hands of the rest of the student population?

ELIZA. First?

How about most recent?

NEIL. Most recent.

ELIZA. Today during lunch Gina Vellenga called me an ugly bitch.

You?

NEIL. On Monday Casey Longo tripped me and said, "Not sorry."

Joy?

JOY. This afternoon.

While newly-crowned Homecoming Queen Brooke Sobota and friends were pre-gaming with Smirnoff Ice, she called me a stupid band geek.

NEIL. Wait.

That's my most recent, too.

Brooke said I was a stupid band geek and that I make her ashamed to be a human.

RUSTY. Who helps us?

ELIZA. No one.

NEIL. No one.

JOY. We only have each other.

ELIZA. Jeff Bird is out there on the football field, a pretty girl on his arm, waving to the crowd.

And you are about to go out there and entertain him.

That is your fate.

RUSTY. You didn't tell me it would be like this.

ELIZA. Yes, we did.

You just didn't believe it.

JOY. Time to lock and load for the halftime show.

(They all strap on their tubas.)

NEIL. What is it this week?

JOY. "Conga" by Gloria Estefan.

> *(They flip through their little sheet music folders.)*

ELIZA. Shoot me.

NEIL. Shoot me and then hang me.

ELIZA. Shoot me and then hang me and then give me an annoying funeral where you play music I didn't even like which speaks to my limited relationship with my mom and say I lit up every room which I didn't and ask everyone to give donations to some charity I mentioned once in passing.

NEIL. Totally.

JOY. Please remember that is a right pinwheel on measure four and full park and bark from measure twelve all the way through measure thirty-two.

ANNOUNCER. Thank you for another great half of East Grand Rapids Pioneer football!

Treat yourself to a bag of popcorn or a cold delicious soda at the snack bar, all proceeds go to the football booster club.

Now sit back, and enjoy the halftime show from the East Grand Rapids Marching Band!!!

> *(The **TUBAS** form a circle, put their hands in the middle.)*

JOY. Crescendo.

ELIZA & NEIL. Crescendo.

JOY. Rusty!

RUSTY. Let me stay here in the bleachers.

JOY. That would look ridiculous.

RUSTY. Jeff Bird is standing right there.

I can't play a halftime show right in front of him.

JOY. And Brooke Sobota is right there, too.

NEIL. I believe I see Chad Venturi laughing like he doesn't have a care in the world.

ELIZA. We all went through what you're going through, Rusty.

When it got real.

Not just an instrument.

A destiny.

JOY. Crescendo.

ELIZA & NEIL. Crescendo!!

ELIZA. This is the price for wanting to appear well-rounded, freshman.

NEIL. I think he peed himself.

ELIZA. Did you pee yourself?

JOY. Eliza, Neil, take the field.

Now!!

ELIZA & NEIL. Crescendo!!!!!!

(**ELIZA** *and* **NEIL** *take the field with a roar.*)

JOY. Did you pee yourself, Rusty?

RUSTY. A little?

JOY. Don't worry.

With the uniforms and the distance, nobody will notice.

RUSTY. Please don't make me go out there, Joy.

JOY. Here's the secret, Rusty.

You told me you're not okay?

JOY. I'm not okay, either.

But I'm here. For you. For Neil and Eliza.

Be here for us, too.

RUSTY. Okay.

JOY. We walk into laughter every Friday night and that's what makes it brave.

RUSTY. But I'm not brave.

JOY. And without forcing yourself to do scary things you never will be.

Crescendo.

RUSTY. Crescendo.

JOY. Crescendo!!

RUSTY. Crescendo!!

(**JOY** *drags* **RUSTY** *onto the field.*)

(*He looks like he's on his way to his own execution.*)

Halftime

(If you haven't looked at the appendix, please do so now. At the end, you'll find different variations on how to handle halftime.)

Wait, Did You Two Just Get Together?

(The following Friday night.)

(An away game. Different stadium. Different bleachers. But because bleachers look exactly the same everywhere, at first you wouldn't know it's an away game.)

(After the halftime show, band members aren't required to wear their full uniforms, so the **TUBA PLAYERS** *are now allowed to have their jackets off.)*

DIFFERENT ANNOUNCER. Fumble recovery by Forest Hills Central, #78, Tom Holodnick.

(The crowd goes wild.)

(The Forest Hills Central band plays a universally recognized stadium chant.)

RUSTY. Why run a halfback sweep when both defensive tackles are lined up on the strong side?

NEIL. Maybe they're trying to exploit the 2–1 no tight end formation?

RUSTY. That's ridiculous.

The defense is in a 4–3 Cover 2.

If we run short curl patterns from the wishbone formation we can exploit their gaping cornerback inexperience and not keep fumbling the ball.

ELIZA. That's a very nuanced reading of the Forest Hills defense, freshman, I applaud you.

DIFFERENT ANNOUNCER. Touchdown, Forest Hills Central!

#33, Michael Morey!!!!

(The crowd goes wild.)

(The Forest Hills Central band plays its fight song.)

ELIZA. It doesn't matter what plays they call.

We suck without Thrillin' Dylan.

NEIL. He blew a .281 for his DUI.

JOY. What????

RUSTY. Is that high?

NEIL. It's three times the legal limit.

JOY. It basically means his heart was pumping lite beer.

NEIL. At the party after the homecoming dance he and A.J. Graham were actually having a contest to see who could blow a higher blood alcohol content.

JOY. Who won?

NEIL. A.J., which means he wasn't driving.

JOY. Dylan threw his future away to beat A.J. in a drinking contest.

NEIL. I'm not angry, I'm disappointed.

JOY. He was already tipsy at the dance.

NEIL. Most of them were.

A very buzzed Jeff Bird tripped over himself attempting the electric slide.

RUSTY. I'm glad Jeff enjoyed himself at least.

NEIL. For a while.

I saw him throw up pork fried rice in the trash can outside the gym.

ELIZA. Ewwwwwww.

JOY. And all the music was sooooo bad.

ELIZA. Bleck.

JOY. Football players can't dance, unilaterally!

NEIL. I was embarrassed on their behalf.

> (**ELIZA**, **JOY**, *and* **NEIL** *mockingly dance like the football players. Calling out their moves such as "The Sprinkler," "Stirring the Porridge," and "Revolving Door."*)

> *(They crack themselves up.)*

But the worst was the slow dancing.

ELIZA. How can anyone take themselves seriously while ass-out slow dancing to a cheesy love song?

> (**JOY** *sings some cheesy high school dance standard while* **ELIZA** *and* **NEIL** *ass-out slow dance. [You know what that means, right? In case not, it's when dance partners push out their butts so as not to encounter their counterpart's nether regions.])*

> *(They crack themselves up again.)*

RUSTY. I'm glad you all had a good time.

ELIZA. Were you able to finish up the paperwork for your Juggling With Clubs merit badge?

RUSTY. Small Boat Sailing, and, yes.

ELIZA. Do you like sailing?

NEIL. I love the wind in my hair and the smell of the sea.

ELIZA. Not you.

RUSTY. I've never been sailing.

ELIZA. You've never even been sailing!

Chalk it up to one more of your completely inauthentic endeavors.

I admire your endurance, freshman.

Bullied, bogus merit badges, a phony political career, peeing your pants before a halftime show, you're putting yourself through a lot of suffering to appear well-rounded.

(Pause.)

RUSTY. My mom calls me her perfect child.

Not in front of my little brother of course.

I learned to walk at the perfect age.

I have the perfect attitude, I get perfect grades.

Parents of my friends compare their own children to me, too.

Being perfect means you have to do a lot of things you wouldn't choose to do on your own.

ELIZA. Like getting beat up and insulted by the entire high school population.

RUSTY. And by members of my own section.

The enemy is out there?

The football players!

The students who call us band geeks!

What about you? How are you any better than the rest of the bullies?

ELIZA. You're a child.

RUSTY. You're fifteen.

ELIZA. You know what I mean.

RUSTY. I'm drowning here. That's no secret.

And yet my presence is the most offensive thing you've ever had to cope with.

You are the single person who makes me feel most worthless, Eliza.

I don't presume to tell you how to live your life but from now on keep your mouth shut about how I live mine.

NEIL. Oh no he didn't.

> (*How will* **ELIZA** *fight back?*)
>
> (**ELIZA** *begins to respond but doesn't know how and runs down the bleachers and exits.*)

Happy?

RUSTY. Satisfied.

From moment one Eliza has done nothing but insult me.

If she can't handle a real argument then she should get off her soapbox and shut up.

JOY. He's got a point, Neil.

NEIL. You don't belong here, freshman!

You're not one of us!!

RUSTY. I never pretended to be!!

NEIL. Quit band! Put down the tuba!! Get off our bleachers!!

RUSTY. This is an away game, these bleachers belong to Forest Hills Central!!

NEIL. You know what I mean, asshole!!*

RUSTY. I do and I won't quit!

---

* Alternatively: **NEIL**. You know what I mean, jerk!!

JOY. Boys!

Enough.

NEIL. Stop playing diplomat, you despise him as much as we do!

JOY. I don't despise him, I pity him.

RUSTY. Oh, thank you, that's so much better.

NEIL. Please, Rusty, don't waste any more time.

Do something for its own sake before it's too late.

(Pause.)

JOY. Did something happen, Neil?

NEIL. My dad died on Wednesday.

RUSTY. Oh my god, I'm so sorry.

JOY. While we were at school?

NEIL. While y'all were eating hot lunch, my mom and I were sitting next to his bed.

We noticed his breath was getting shallower and shallower.

When the nurse came in she took one look and said, "Your father is actively dying."

"Actively dying." Those two words didn't make any sense put together.

I asked how long he had. She said, "Not long."

"Hours?"

"Minutes."

RUSTY. Woah.

NEIL. Woah is right.

The second hand on the clock suddenly becomes a different proposition when there are only a few ticks of it left.

NEIL. My mom and I looked at each other, like we just got to that freaky first climb of a roller coaster when you know you're about go over the top and there's nothing you can do about it except scream.

We sat on either side of the bed, both of us held one of his hands, we whispered into his ears: "You lived a good life. You can rest now."

His breath got shallower and shallower and shallower.

There was no final gasp so we weren't sure if he was still alive; we whispered for the other person to put their finger under his nose to see if he was still breathing.

"You do it."

"No, you do it."

I finally did it and my finger started shaking I held it there so long.

When I was sure he was gone I closed his eyes like in the movies but they popped right back open again.

JOY. He was alive???

(**ELIZA** *has returned, unseen, she's listening.*)

NEIL. No.

Dead people's eyes open like that. The hospice nurse told us that later.

They put a sheet over him, and we put his glasses and wallet in a plastic bag.

It's only me and my mom and there's so much to take care of so I've been driving his car to do errands.

His dry cleaning is still in the back and these peppermint breath mints I hate are in the drink holder.

An old newspaper down in the trunk for muddy shoes.

ELIZA. When you gave me a ride home yesterday were we in your dad's car?

NEIL. And the breath mint you declined was also his.

(**JOY** *and* **RUSTY** *share a look.*)

("Did you know they were hanging out just the two of them?")

ELIZA. I was surprised you had them in the first place.

NEIL. Because I have bad breath?

ELIZA. No.

Peppermint just didn't feel like you.

I'm sorry you've had to go through this, Neil.

It's so much to process on your own.

(**ELIZA** *holds* **NEIL**'s *hand.*)

(Is it romantic?)

(Is it a consoling friend?)

(A bit of both?)

(**ELIZA** *buries her head in* **NEIL**'s *shoulder.*)

JOY. Wait, did you two just get together?

NEIL. I hope so?

ELIZA. Yes.

We did.

NEIL. Oh, wow.

(**NEIL** *smiles from the inside.*)

(They all watch the game.)

(**NEIL** *and* **ELIZA** *hold hands.*)

(**NEIL** *buries his head in* **ELIZA**'s *shoulder.*)

(Both of their lives just shifted.)

*(**JOY** and **RUSTY** know both of their lives just shifted and share a silent "oh my god," and "shhhhh, don't ruin it.")*

(They all watch the game for a while.)

(The roar of the crowd.)

*(**JOY** and **RUSTY** are thrilled for the world's newest couple.)*

*(**ELIZA** and **NEIL** are a million miles away, occupants of their own world.)*

Somewhere Safe

(A few weeks later.)

(A high school football stadium.)

(The bleachers.)

(During the day.)

(Lunch.)

*(**RUSTY** does his homework and eats a sandwich from his superhero lunchbox.)*

*(**NEIL** approaches.)*

*(**RUSTY** doesn't want to be interrupted.)*

NEIL. Hey.

RUSTY. Hey.

NEIL. Do you come here often?

I've always wanted to say that.

RUSTY. Often enough.

(Pause.)

NEIL. Like right now.

RUSTY. Apparently.

(Pause.)

NEIL. Why?

RUSTY. Why what?

NEIL. Why do you come to the bleachers often enough?

RUSTY. It's quiet.

NEIL. Space to think.

RUSTY. It's a good place to do homework.

NEIL. Is that what you're doing right now?

RUSTY. No, I'm just looking at this textbook for fun.

NEIL. Yeah, sometimes I do the same.

    (Silence.)

What kind of homework?

RUSTY. English.

NEIL. Ahhhhhh.

A worthy subject.

    (Silence.)

    (RUSTY *works.)*

Big test coming up?

RUSTY. Big-ish.

NEIL. Good thing you're studying.

    (Pause.)

Studying is really important.

    (Pause.)

If your goal is to do well.

RUSTY. Is there something you want to talk about?

NEIL. No.

You?

RUSTY. No.

NEIL. Then I'll just let you get back to it.

RUSTY. Thank you.

> *(Silence.)*

> *(**RUSTY** works.)*

Maybe I come to the bleachers to avoid certain people.

NEIL. Sometimes I think if I sit here long enough I'll become part of the aluminum.

> *(Pause.)*

Which certain people?

RUSTY. I think you know.

NEIL. I think I can guess but I don't think I know, not for certain, nothing is certain.

RUSTY. Then guess.

NEIL. Jeff Bird.

RUSTY. Bingo.

NEIL. It really is a blessing Chad Venturi isn't your bully, because he is pretty much a felon.

RUSTY. Yeah, I thank my lucky stars every day.

NEIL. Gratitude.

They say it's the key to happiness.

Or peace, I should say.

Because happiness comes and goes.

I guess everything comes and goes.

Do you ever think you're dead and this is hell?

RUSTY. No.

NEIL. Oh.

> *(Pause.)*

Sometimes I do.

(**RUSTY** *sighs,* **NEIL** *isn't going anywhere.*)

NEIL. Life stopped feeling real.

After my dad.

We put him in the ground.

And every day since then I wonder if I'm alive or not.

And if I am, if I'm in heaven or hell.

Because if you were in hell wouldn't it be even worse if nobody told you you were dead?

RUSTY. Are you okay?

NEIL. No?

RUSTY. There are people you can talk to.

NEIL. I'm talking to you.

RUSTY. Professionals.

NEIL. No, thanks.

RUSTY. I've been going to a therapist for almost two years.

NEIL. Oh.

RUSTY. For anxiety.

(*Silence.*)

I have crippling anxiety.

NEIL. About what?

RUSTY. About being perfect.

NEIL. You're not.

RUSTY. Thank you.

NEIL. No one is.

RUSTY. Which is what my therapist says.

He tells me I can just take it slow and enjoy my life and I'm like, my parents are paying you $125 an hour to tell me to enjoy my life?

But I'm like take it easy?

To get where I want to go I need a 4.0 and fantastic test scores.

I already have an SAT tutor.

NEIL. You're a freshman.

RUSTY. But the fall of junior year is the PSAT and it's the first indication if you're going to be a special kid or not.

National Merit Semi-Finalist.

Because if you're not one then goodbye Ivy Leagues.

NEIL. I was one of those.

RUSTY. You were?

NEIL. I think so.

RUSTY. What was your SAT score?

NEIL. I don't remember.

Wait.

3432.

No. That's my mom's personal identification number, forget you heard that.

1540 on my SAT.

Is that a number people get?

Is that a number people get?

RUSTY. 1540???

That's like top one percent in the nation!

NEIL. Yeah, that's what I got.

RUSTY. You're like a genius.

NEIL. Yeah.

>   (*Pause.*)

I'll let you get back to it.

>   (*He doesn't go anywhere.*)

RUSTY. You're not in hell.

NEIL. Are you sure?

RUSTY. Pretty sure.

NEIL. Because how would we know the difference?

Einstein said if you could move at the speed of light everything else would be a memory.

And I wonder if this is happening or it happened forever ago and we're not really here at all.

RUSTY. Can I give you the number of my therapist, Neil?

NEIL. Yeah, that sounds like maybe it's a good idea.

>   (**JOY** *arrives.*)

JOY. Well well well.

The bleachers have become somewhere safe for you, too.

RUSTY. I'm probably more surprised than anyone.

JOY. You ready for your music lesson?

NEIL. No, thanks.

JOY. For him.

NEIL. Ahhhhh.

That makes more sense.

JOY. Where were we, Rusty?

RUSTY. The circle of fifths.

NEIL. Ahhhh.

The circle of fifths.

> (**NEIL** *has nothing more to say about that, he lets it drift into silence.*)

JOY. Neil.

NEIL. What?

JOY. You know what.

NEIL. I can guess what, I can't know anything, not for certain.

JOY. Maybe you could sit somewhere else.

NEIL. I could also stand somewhere else, too.

Or dance somewhere else. Sing. Nap.

If I happened to be a napper.

> (*Pause.*)

Which I'm not.

My dad was.

Huge napper.

JOY. Is there something you'd like to talk about?

NEIL. No.

You?

JOY. I'd like to talk about the circle of fifths.

NEIL. Who's stopping you?

JOY. You are.

NEIL. The circle of fifths.

Counterpoint, polyrhythm, consonant harmony.

NEIL. Yes, you can study music, but maybe instead study reality as music, because our world is a series of fundamental vibrations.

You want to know why I really joined band?

RUSTY. I would love to know.

JOY. I would, too.

NEIL. The real reason I joined band was because Johannes Kepler said that every time humans play or listen to music we imitate God.

JOY. Okay, that's definitely not what I thought you were going to say.

NEIL. When Kepler found out that planets move in ellipses and not circles, he put the relative velocities of our planets next to the intervals of a violin and he got a C major chord.

What????

Kepler kept writing laws of planetary motion and expanded the voices of the planets.

From notes to melodies, each tone represented a different speed at various points on their orbits.

I had to find out how that was possible.

So I joined band, and found out music isn't a subject it's my proof of God.

And the more I learned about that way of life the more I realized that what I want to do with my life is to help people hear the perfect singing in the spheres of heaven.

RUSTY. Thrillin' Dylan really does have a fantastic deal on his math homework.

      (**ELIZA** *arrives.*)

ELIZA. Hey.

JOY & RUSTY. Hey.

NEIL. Are you here for the music lesson, too?

ELIZA. No, I'm here to pick you up.

NEIL. Which makes a lot more sense.

ELIZA. What are you two studying?

NEIL. They were attempting to study the circle of fifths but I'm talking about reality as a series of fundamental vibrations.

ELIZA. We've got to get going, pookie.

NEIL. Pookie?

ELIZA. I'm trying it out.

What do you think?

JOY. I don't really like it.

RUSTY. Neil doesn't feel like a pookie.

NEIL. Pookie.

Pookie.

I like it better than stud muffin.

ELIZA. Then let's get going, pookie.

JOY. Where are you two going?

NEIL. Third base for sure.

Maybe the whole shaboodle, depending on the breaks.

ELIZA. Pookie!!

NEIL. Who's Pookie?

ELIZA. Go!

NEIL. Enjoy your music lesson, Rusty.

When you allow for the possibility that when we make music we imitate God your life will never be the same.

(**NEIL** *bows and goes.*)

ELIZA. Sorry about him.

JOY. Don't be.

RUSTY. Grief.

ELIZA. Grief.

(*Pause.*)

Did Neil tell you he got into MIT?

RUSTY. The Massachusetts Institute of Technology?

ELIZA. Early decision!!

RUSTY. Why didn't he say something?

ELIZA.   Probably because external validation and achievement don't define his self-worth.

But that's just a guess.

NEIL. (*Offstage.*) Let's go, sweetums!!

ELIZA. Nope, not that one, either!!

RUSTY. Tell him congratulations.

JOY. From both of us. It's a huge accomplishment.

ELIZA. We're going to celebrate! See you before the game tonight.

JOY. 5:30 uniforms on and ready for inspection.

ELIZA. Yes, Section Leader.

JOY. Sorry, I can't turn it off.

NEIL. (*Offstage.*) Love muffin!!!

ELIZA. I'm coming!!!

(**ELIZA** *goes.*)

JOY. So. The circle of fifths.

Starting with the five-note Pythagorean pentatonic scale: Do Re Mi Sol La –

RUSTY. – am I living a good life?

JOY. As your marching band section leader, I don't think I'm qualified to answer that question.

RUSTY. Who is?

JOY. You.

(Pause.)

You're brave, Rusty.

RUSTY. Then why do I feel so scared?

JOY. Because being scared is right where you're supposed to be.

Brave isn't before fear, it's what comes after.

You got this.

RUSTY. "Fake it till you make it."

JOY. Exactly.

Until then, the circle of fifths.

When you fully grasp it, you'll understand how a simple series of vibrations in the air help us write the emotional story of our lives...

(The lights fade.)

The Last Game

(It's really cold in the bleachers.)

(The **TUBA PLAYERS** *have to blow into their mouthpieces from time to time to keep them from freezing and press the valves a bunch to make sure they don't get stuck from the cold.)*

ANNOUNCER. As we say farewell to another season of high school football, East Grand Rapids Football Boosters ask you to salute the twenty-two departing seniors for all their effort and excellence.

(The crowd applauds.)

*(***ELIZA, RUSTY,** *and* **JOY** *all applaud* **NEIL.***)*

(He bows.)

ELIZA. Thank you for your effort, departing senior!

JOY. Thank you for your excellence!

ELIZA. Speech!

ELIZA, JOY & RUSTY. Speech!! Speech!!

NEIL. Sitting in these bleachers has provided my view of high school.

When I look back on my adolescence I'll picture this.

I'll picture all of you.

ELIZA, JOY & RUSTY. Awwwwwww.

ANNOUNCER. And let's especially salute our fallen hero Scott Griffin.

Welcome back, Scott!!!

(The crowd applauds louder.)

RUSTY. Scott looks horrible.

NEIL. He almost had to have his left leg amputated.

JOY. What??

NEIL. My mom saw his mom crying in the international foods aisle of the supermarket.

My dad's birthday is coming up and his favorite night was taco night but that doesn't matter it's not part of the story, the initial surgery went well but in the middle of the night one week later Scott felt an extreme pressure in his leg, which came to be known as Acute Compartment Syndrome, a surgical emergency that must be dealt with immediately but it was the middle of the night and Scott didn't want to go the emergency room, who does, right, and by the time Scott was seen by his doctor the next morning the pressure within his osteofascial compartment was so far along that they were able to save the leg, barely, but it will never fully recover.

(They look at **NEIL**.*)*

What?

My dad was an orthopedic surgeon.

RUSTY. Scott will never play football again.

NEIL. Scott will never walk normally again.

ELIZA. What has Scott done with the gift?

The uniform will never go back on, what has he found so far?

*(***JOY*** breaks down crying.)*

Joy, what's wrong?

JOY. My mom saw a hickey on my neck.

She asked where I got it and I told her from a girl.

JOY. My mom said I am her view into the heart of God but if I'm gay she won't be able to see God anymore.

(**ELIZA** *grabs* **JOY** *close and holds her.*)

(**ELIZA** *wants to squeeze* **JOY** *so tight that all her fear and pain would go away but you never can squeeze anybody that tight no matter how much you try.*)

I love going to church.

I love our community.

I love God unconditionally.

How can I reconcile the God I love with the one she says hates me for who I am?

NEIL. Who gave you the hickey?

ELIZA. Neil!!

NEIL. What??

It's integral to the story!

JOY. Sadie gave it to me.

NEIL. Your proof of God from the gas station outside the wanky music festival?

JOY. I drove back and found her.

There were three customers before me in line, I was sure my heart was going to burst out of my chest.

When she asked how she could help me I blurted "by saying you remember me."

RUSTY. Did she?

JOY. Not in the slightest.

I'm another anonymous customer.

But she remembered the luna moth.

I told her what that night did to me, her eyes.

Sadie took me back to her parents' house where we watched bad music videos and made out all night in her basement.

NEIL. Go get it, girl.

JOY. I called my mom to say I was spending the night at your house, Eliza.

I hope that's okay.

ELIZA. You can always use me as your excuse, you know that.

JOY. The next morning.

My eyes opened, and seeing Sadie's face inches from mine, it's the happiest I've ever been in my life.

I didn't want to breathe, I just wanted to keep looking at her as long as I could.

She finally woke up and had to get to work.

I drove home, I couldn't stop smiling.

When my mom saw the hickey I told her the truth.

Now my parents are sending me to a conversion camp in Minnesota where they pray-the-gay-away.

ELIZA. They can't do that.

JOY. I'm sixteen years old.

I can't bar the door to my bedroom.

I don't have another legal residence.

ELIZA. Come live with me, Joy.

JOY. Are you serious?

ELIZA. My mom would be thrilled.

It's just the two of us, she always wanted another child.

JOY. But I have a duty to my family.

ELIZA. And you have a duty to yourself.

Your real self, not what you've been conditioned to believe is right or wrong.

You need the space to find out who you are.

Let me give it to you, Joy.

JOY. Okay.

ELIZA. Yes?

JOY. Yes.

ANNOUNCER. And it would be a crime to not give a special sendoff to a once in a generation football player, Thrillin' Dylan Anderson!!

Who finished his playing career only twelve touchdowns shy of the Michigan High School record.

(The crowd roars.)

Dylan isn't able to play in the game tonight, but let's hear the fight song played for him, one last time.

ELIZA. Seriously?

JOY. Mr. Papalko didn't say anything to me.

ANNOUNCER. The East Grand Rapids Marching Band invites you to sing along to the fight song, "Onward East High!"

NEIL.

Once more, unto the breach, dear friends, once more:

Or close the wall up with our English dead.

(Lights shift. The four **BAND MEMBERS** *become their adult selves.)*

ADULT ELIZA. *(To us.)* During high school I imagined I was practicing invisibility so I could survive the rest of my life.

But now I know that I was studying.

How people move.

How they look when they almost say something real and then swallow it.

It's been thirty years since I graduated and everything I learned about how to read the world began from looking at it for four years of sitting here.

All I wanted to be was Tuba Player #3. Instead? I became the star of my life, lit from within.

I didn't know that I was building my entire sense of resilience on the back of four years no one clapped for.

This fight song is supposed to belong to the football players.

Turns out we're the ones worth fighting for.

ADULT RUSTY. *(To us.)* I remember thinking East Grand Rapids was the smallest place I'd ever live.

That I'd outgrow it like a shoe someone who had no idea who I was picked out for me.

Three decades later I still dream about this view.

About these nights.

Crisp fall air.

Popcorn.

I still dream about what it felt like to live in the background of someone else's story.

I took my place in the bleachers to look like someone.

A perfect child, a résumé in human form.

Instead of becoming perfect I became real.

ADULT NEIL. *(To us.)* It still haunts me in my dreams, the announcer, "East Grand Rapids Touchdown, #24 Thrillin' Dylan Anderson!!!!"

My body sat here for four years, slowly dissolving into this aluminum bench, entertaining an indifferent to outright hostile crowd.

I didn't know that marching across a field while the whole town laughed prepared me to walk into rooms where no one expected me to belong and sit down like I did.

This place, these friends, they helped build the scaffolding of who I would evolve into.

ADULT JOY. *(To us.)* I was loud because I was scared.

Because if I stopped shouting counts and getting it right, someone might ask me who I really was.

And I wasn't ready to say it.

But I loved this place.

God, I did.

When I played music, like really played, it became like a transmission.

Like I was sending signals through the instrument just to see who's actually listening.

These three lovely humans are the ones who spoke in static, too.

I didn't know that they would be the ones I still ask when I need to remember who I was before I became what the world asked for.

ADULT ELIZA. How's your knee, by the way?

ADULT JOY. I can still tell when it's going to rain.

ADULT NEIL. Does your knee have any feelings about next Thursday?

I've got a thing outside that I hope gets cancelled.

ADULT JOY. You'll be the first to know.

ADULT RUSTY. *(To us.)* Back in high school I didn't know I'd found the first group of people who let me be exactly as I am. Right here.

In the last place I wanted to be, in the back row of the bleachers.

My tuba section showed me what courage is.

Because it's easy to walk into a stadium full of cheers and applause.

But it takes bravery to walk into laughter and to stay anyway.

(Lights shift.)

(The four **TUBAS** *return to their high school selves and the last game of the season.)*

JOY. Is Thrillin' Dylan crying?

ELIZA. I believe that's called weeping.

NEIL. Or keening, depending on your cultural milieu.

RUSTY. An American tragedy in real time.

NEIL. All the Division I schools dropped him.

RUSTY. What???

NEIL. For his probation he was assigned twenty-four hours of community service and Dylan didn't bother to show up so he spent five days in jail.

RUSTY. He won't get a scholarship anywhere?

NEIL. Would you want a kid who has two arrests and doesn't have the wherewithal to show up for his community service to represent your university?

ELIZA. So probably just Dylan from now on.

RUSTY. Thrillin' no more.

JOY. We witnessed it.

The greatest moment of Dylan's life.

NEIL. At seventeen years old.

JOY. Homecoming King.

Three touchdowns in the first half alone.

Colleges drooling over him.

Girls wanting him, boys wanting to be him.

The dreams of a community on his shoulders.

And now mortality, and regret.

NEIL. I can't believe I'm saying this, but I feel bad for Dylan.

RUSTY. He beat the crap out of you and made you do his math homework.

NEIL. Yeah, but he sort of played it up, like he was a person who understood that this was his role.

High school hero.

It's like how you want a rock star to be totally self-destructive and knee-deep into heroin and STDs because they're fulfilling the contract of their role when they do and it's like kind of unnatural when they're some goody-two-shoes loser who is out there playing music for the love of it.

You want to see your rock and roll heroes live the self-destruction they espouse.

And Thrillin' Dylan?

Every inch his role.

He took it on completely, consciously or not, no one can say.

But he dated the most popular girl in school, he made fun of band geeks, bullied us, and exploited his public image to court favor from teachers and the administration.

And every week he lived up to his hype.

I've watched every single football game of his since I blocked a tackle for him in middle school.

His athletic ability was a true gift.

And now that gift is gone.

(**ELIZA** *takes her boyfriend's hand.*)

ELIZA. Tonight those twenty-two young men leave their time under the lights, after four more quarters their lives will begin to decline, and your life will begin to flourish.

(*A kiss.*)

RUSTY. Congratulations on getting into MIT, Neil.

It's a huge accomplishment.

ELIZA. An accomplishment which you are in part responsible for, freshman.

RUSTY. Me?

NEIL. I put in my early decision application Monday morning after the first football game because I was like, if that phony asshole can get into a good college I can, too.[*]

RUSTY. You're welcome?

ELIZA. Your dad would be so proud of you.

NEIL. Yeah?

RUSTY. You're going to the best science and technology university in the country, if not the world.

If there's a heaven your dad is grinning ear to ear.

---

[*] Alternatively: **NEIL**. ...if that phony loser can get into a good college I can, too.

NEIL. Oh, wow.

JOY. I can really tell my parents I'm staying with you tonight, Eliza?

ELIZA. You can tell your parents you're staying with me indefinitely.

JOY. You're sure your mom will be okay with it.

ELIZA. When I get in a dark mood she hovers like a wasp at a picnic and I want to scream.

Having my best friend there would make her life easier.

JOY. Could we go by my house and get some essentials after the game?

ELIZA. Or if you'd rather not see your family right now you can have whatever you need.

Toothbrush.

Pajamas.

> (**JOY** *hugs* **ELIZA**.)

We're your family, too.

JOY. And I thank God for it.

RUSTY. How dark do your moods get, Eliza?

ELIZA. Why do you want to know?

NEIL. Because Rusty's been going to a therapist for over two years for anxiety.

RUSTY. Thank you for telling everyone.

NEIL. No need to thank me.

RUSTY. I'm not.

NEIL. Dr. Shahibi has been really helpful, though. I never said thank you for putting us in touch.

RUSTY. You didn't say you started seeing him.

NEIL. Because I wanted it to remain private.

RUSTY. So did I.

NEIL. I understand the feeling.

JOY. You've been going to therapy for two years?

NEIL. No, I've only been a few times.

ELIZA. Not you.

NEIL. Sorry, Love.

> *(Pause.)*

Right?

> *(**ELIZA** accepts the nickname.)*

ELIZA. Yes, Love.

JOY. You have anxiety, Rusty.

NEIL. Crippling.

RUSTY. What he said.

JOY. So do I.

NEIL. Not me.

Dr. Shahibi says I just need time to adjust to a world where there was a soul and now an empty space.

ELIZA. How dark do my moods get?

At five years old I got in fights with other kids.

By seven even the boys in the neighborhood were terrified of me.

I would throw myself on the floor and scream when I didn't get what I wanted, I would roll onto my back and beat myself in the face.

It only got worse as I got older.

My mom took me to every type of therapy in existence.

ELIZA. Cognitive, gestalt, somatic, rational emotive behavior therapy.

Even equine assisted therapy.

NEIL. There's nothing like the sweat on a mare after a proper canter.

ELIZA. Nothing worked.

She gave up.

But one morning we were in the car, my mom was flipping through stations and when I heard The Beatles I sat still for the first time in my life.

Music gets me through the day.

For me it's the only power on this earth that has the ability to quiet the rage inside me and order the static in my head.

That's why I joined band, to get to be inside my favorite thing in the universe.

And you're here, a total phony, using God's gift of music to look like Mommy's perfect child.

RUSTY. That's it.

I quit.

JOY. We only have four more quarters, you can make it, little buddy.

RUSTY. Not band.

Boy Scouts.

> (**RUSTY** *takes out his Boy Scout sash with merit badges sewn into it.*)

NEIL. You carry your Boy Scout sash with you wherever you go?

RUSTY. We're supposed to leave on a camping trip after the game tonight.

But I hate camping.

I hate the cold, the bugs, the food, the smell of fire, the sounds of nature.

NEIL. Yeah, camping might not be for you.

RUSTY. I'm not going camping tonight or ever again.

> (**RUSTY** *rips off the merit badges one by one and hands them to* **ELIZA**.)

Animal Science. Wilderness Survival. Fingerprinting. Small Boat Sailing.

NEIL. Can I get Basketry?

RUSTY. It's yours.

NEIL. Score.

RUSTY. Coin Collecting. Fire Safety. Dentistry.

JOY. They teach Dentistry in Boy Scouts?

RUSTY. I had to make a model tooth out of soap and demonstrate proper flossing procedures.

NEIL. I would benefit from that particular tutorial.

RUSTY. Leatherwork. Landscape Architecture. Automotive Maintenance. Archery.

Woodcarving. Animal Science, avian option.

NEIL. Does that mean you can do bird calls?

RUSTY. Hell yes it does. Close your eyes.

> (**JOY** *and* **NEIL** *close their eyes.*)

> (**RUSTY** *does a meadowlark call.*)

NEIL. A red breasted meadowlark, you have a gift.

ELIZA. Quitting Boy Scouts.

Wow.

ELIZA. The revolution has begun.

RUSTY. And I resign my presidency of the freshman class.

JOY. Do we need to alert the vice president now or can it wait until Monday?

NEIL. My cousin's a notary public if you need official documentation.

RUSTY. Boy Scouts, my student council presidency.

And I quit Latin Club, yearbook and Safety Town, too.

ELIZA. How will any child cross the street ever again?

RUSTY. They'll figure it out because Safety Town is a lie!!

I'm a complete phony!

ELIZA. Which I've been saying since the beginning.

RUSTY. And I'm the last person to realize you're right.

NEIL. What about the newspaper and the environmental club?

RUSTY. You see? Those clubs are such lies I don't even remember being in them!

They're gone, too!

JOY. It doesn't make sense to throw away all that hard work, Rusty.

RUSTY. You're right!

It doesn't!

Maybe all this pressure I put on myself is the gift. But what have I done with it?

NEIL. Will you do the meadowlark again?

(**RUSTY** *does the meadowlark again.*)

Like the singing in the spheres!

RUSTY. Jeff Bird!!!!

You're nothing but a Tier II bully!!!! You hear me??

JOY. The game hasn't started, he can definitely hear you.

RUSTY. I'm coming for you tonight because I know where you live!!!!

NEIL. I guess someone does care where Jeff Bird lives.

ELIZA. What are you going to tell Mommy and Daddy?

RUSTY. That I'm not their perfect child.

But I might be something even better.

> *(Pause.)*

ELIZA. What are you doing after the game tonight?

JOY. No more merit badges.

NEIL. No more emergency meetings in the student council situation room.

RUSTY. For the first time in my life I have absolutely no idea what I'm doing.

ELIZA. Maybe we could all do something together.

NEIL. I could drive.

> *(They look at him.)*

My mom's car. We sold my dad's.

If you ever want an easy time at a car dealership, call and say you're selling the vehicle of a newly deceased family member. We handed over the keys, received embarrassed condolences, a check and walked right out. Quicker than a rental car return.

RUSTY. Maybe after the game I could help transport your essentials to your new home.

JOY. That sounds perfect.

NEIL. Welcome to the Untouchables.

RUSTY. What does it say about me to be accepted as an outcast of outcasts?

JOY. It means no matter how screwed up you are you always have a home.

ELIZA. Welcome home, Rusty.

ANNOUNCER. Football season goes so fast. Let's join voices for one final night.

East Grand Rapids to kick off from their own 25-yard line.

> (**EVERYONE** *stomps the bleachers, holds their hands above their heads, wiggles their fingers and says, "Aaaaaaaaaaaahhhh" until the ball is kicked, and they all drop their hands and say:)*

ALL. Crescendo!!

> *(The* **TUBA PLAYERS** *pick up their tubas and for the first time we get to hear them play music. Whatever song speaks to the students working on your production. If you have a* **CHORUS**, *they enter playing instruments. Stagehands can enter playing instruments. Ushers, choreographers, hair and makeup, everybody who worked on* Bleachers *in your high school can enter playing an instrument. You can play off-key. On key. Somewhere in between, who cares, as long as you play it loud.)*
>
> *(The lights grow ever brighter on the true heroes of Friday night football games.)*

End of Play

APPENDIX: CHORAL BEATS

Grouped by theme, use some, use none, splice them together, double the voices, triple them, write your own, have fun.

What It Feels Like To Watch Football Players Applauded While We Get Laughed At

VOICE ONE. It feels like wearing armor you weren't invited to battle in.

VOICE TWO. Like being part of the ritual but never the myth.

VOICE THREE. Like yelling instructions while everyone yells something else louder.

And then realizing your voice was never part of the sound system.

VOICE FOUR. It feels like being good.

So good.

Sharp lines.

Clean sets.

No mistakes.

And then hearing someone in the third row say, "What are they even doing out there?"

VOICE FIVE. It feels like we don't get remembered.

But we do get watched.

Every step, every note, every fall.

Laughed at, but still showing up in front of the entire town.

Like it's a stage we weren't supposed to step onto.

VOICE SIX. We don't get cheered.

But we still go out there.

That's what makes it brave.

That's what makes it ours.

Where I Go In My Mind When I'm Playing

VOICE ONE. I go to a version of this town where no one's watching but everyone's listening.

VOICE TWO. I got a memory that hasn't happened yet.

Me, on a stage I've never seen, playing something I haven't written.

But it knows me.

VOICE THREE. I go nowhere.

That's the best part.

It's the only time I'm not thinking.

Just...vibrating.

VOICE FOUR. I go back to my grandfather's garage.

He used to whistle while fixing things.

When I play, I feel like I'm answering him.

VOICE FIVE. I go under the bleachers.

Not in real life.

In my head.

Where I can cry if I need to and come back in on the count of four.

VOICE SIX. I go into the bell of my instrument.

Like I live there.

Like if you looked inside, you'd see my whole life folded up into sound.

VOICE SEVEN. When I'm playing, I'm somewhere else.

But also, I'm the most here I'll ever be.

VOICE ONE. I go where no one claps but I still feel heard.

Arts Are Essential, Athletics Are Diversion

VOICE ONE. You build a stadium before you build a stage.

And then you tell us the arts are optional.

VOICE TWO. You cheer for touchdowns like they feed your soul.

But when we make music you treat us like decoration.

Like filler.

Like something to kill time between real events.

VOICE THREE. You teach kids how to win before you teach them how to express sorrow.

How to listen.

How to make beauty out of pressure instead of violence.

VOICE FOUR. Athletics distract.

Arts reveal.

VOICE FIVE. You say it's tradition.

But you only pass down the rituals that make noise.

Not the ones that make sense.

VOICE SIX. We're not jealous.

We're just tired of being called enrichment when we are the language people come back to when they don't know how to keep breathing.

VOICE SEVEN. Arts and athletics both have value.

But only one teaches you how to speak when the game ends and the silence starts.

The First Time A Football Player Bullied Me

VOICE ONE. It wasn't physical.

He said, "Nobody cares if you're here."

And I believed him for a whole year.

VOICE TWO. He slapped my music out of my hands.

"Oops."

I picked it up.

He walked away like it never happened.

It still happens every time I see his number on the back of a jersey, #20.

VOICE THREE. He called me "band bitch" in the locker.

Laughed.

His friends laughed, too.

I laughed it off.

Because if you don't laugh you give them what they want: a reaction.

VOICE FOUR. He pushed my clarinet off the bleachers.

It cracked.

He said, "You should thank me, now you don't have to play."

VOICE FIVE. I don't remember his name.

But I remember the sound of everyone pretending they didn't hear it happen.

What Spending High School In The Bleachers Teaches You About Love

VOICE ONE. Love is showing up even when you're not the reason people came.

VOICE TWO. Love is playing your part with all you've got, knowing they won't clap your name and doing it anyway.

VOICE THREE. Love is watching someone fall apart mid-song and catching them without words.

VOICE FOUR. Love is tuning to each other in the middle of a hundred distractions and finding the same note.

VOICE FIVE. Love is the silence between songs when no one's looking and someone says, "That was really good."

VOICE SIX. Love is showing up again the next Friday.

And the next.

And the next.

Even if it rained.

Even if it hurt.

Even if you didn't feel like you were enough.

Because someone else might need you there.

Even if they never say it.

Who I Was Before Band

VOICE ONE. I used to fake stomachaches to get out of gym.

Not because I hated sports.

Because I didn't know how to enter a room.

VOICE TWO. I was the kid who read the backs of cereal boxes three times.

Because no one talked at breakfast.

And the words didn't mind being read again.

VOICE THREE. I was loud.

Too loud.

I didn't know where to put all the noise.

Band gave me a container.

VOICE FOUR. I was nothing special.

Not bad. Not good.

Just...kind of the background.

Band taught me how to take up space without apologizing.

VOICE FIVE. I used to think belonging was for people who looked like they had somewhere else to go.

I never did.

Then one day, someone handed me a pair of gloves and said, "You're late."

And I wasn't.

VOICE SIX. Before band, I didn't know how to breathe on purpose.

VOICE ONE. I didn't know who I was.

But I showed up.

And something met me there.

VOICE TWO. I wasn't a musician yet.

VOICE THREE. I wasn't seen yet.

But I was becoming.

What I Wish I'd Said Before The Last Song (From The Future Looking Back)

VOICE ONE. I wish I'd said thank you.

Not to the director.

To the kid who stood next to me for four years and always whispered, "You got this," right before the downbeat.

VOICE TWO. I wish I'd said, "Please don't leave yet."

Even if we were never that close.

Even if it would've made it weird.

VOICE THREE. I wish I'd said, "This was the first place I ever felt like I was part of the rhythm."

I didn't say anything.

I just nodded and packed up my case like it was just another Tuesday.

VOICE FOUR. I wish I'd told her I remembered her solo from sophomore year.

That it made me cry and I pretended it was allergies.

VOICE FIVE. I wish I'd said, "I'm proud of you."

To myself.

Out loud.

Even just once.

VOICE SIX. I wish I'd said, "Let's play it again.

One more time.

Not for the crowd.

For us."

What I Would Say To Him Now
(From The Future Looking Back)

VOICE ONE. I'd say

"You didn't break me."

Even though you tried.

Even though I let you think you did.

VOICE TWO. I'd say

I'm still here.

Still playing.

Still marching.

Still me.

Which is more than you ever bothered to see.

VOICE THREE. I'd say

"I hope you grew up."

I really do.

Because being seventeen is no excuse for teaching someone to hate themselves.

VOICE FOUR. I wouldn't scream.

I'd look you in the eye and say, "You were wrong about me."

VOICE FIVE. I'd say

"You made me smaller."

Then I'd pause.

Then I'd add,

"But only for a little while."

VOICE SIX. I wouldn't say anything.

I'd just play.

Loud.

On-key.

Facing the crowd with my back to you.

What I Never Got To Play
(From The Future Looking Back)

VOICE ONE. I practiced that solo every night for two weeks.

Alone.

In the garage.

I still know it by heart.

VOICE TWO. There was a piece we played through only once.

It had this one chord, in measure 47.

When we hit it in rehearsal, I closed my eyes.

Just for a second.

It felt like my head was the center of the universe.

We cut the song the next day.

VOICE THREE. I wanted to write something.

An arrangement.

A new fight song.

I started it on a napkin once.

But I never showed anyone.

Because I didn't think I was allowed to compose.

VOICE FOUR. There's a love song I always hoped would sneak into the set list.

Not because I believed in the words.

Because I wanted to know what it felt like to play something soft and be taken seriously.

VOICE FIVE. I never got to play what I sound like when no one was watching.

VOICE SIX. I never got to play the version of me that wasn't trying to be good.

Just…honest.

The Last Song
(What It Feels Like When It Ends)

VOICE ONE. The last note didn't echo. It just stopped.

And the silence was so loud it filled my whole body.

VOICE TWO. I kept my uniform in the closet for a year.

Like maybe they'd ask me back.

VOICE THREE. The field lights went out.

But I still saw the path I marched every week.

My feet remembered.

VOICE FOUR. I miss the applause I never got.

Because I gave everything.

And left nothing behind.

VOICE FIVE. The last song wasn't for the crowd.

It was for us.

For who we were.

For who we became.

Halftime Options

OPTION ONE:

Nothing. Intermission. Take a break. Phew.

OPTION TWO:

Choreograph your own halftime show using as many of the lyrics on the next page or lyrics you write yourselves in any order and echoed as needed. They can be whispered, chanted, or sung-spoken, like found poetry. You can march in formations. You can stand bolt upright. You can work under weird, shadow-y lights or full-on blazing stadium lights. Rusty, Eliza, Joy and Neil can be part of your halftime show, or you can leave it just to the Chorus. Make it yours in every way. Every football halftime show since time immemorial has been designed to entertain the crowd. The halftime show you create for *BLEACHERS* has the single goal of self-expression.

OPTION THREE:

Some totally original concept I haven't imagined that you create and which I absolutely cannot wait to see.

Lyrics

My solo was silence, and no one applauded.

I marched in time but cried in rests.

I know every measure of someone else's anthem.

My instrument never fit right, but I played anyway.

I kept showing up. That's how I made a sound.

I learned to hold the silence as tightly as the note.

I tuned to people who never heard me.

This field was never level, and still I ran.

I danced while holding in a scream.

I wasn't the background. I was the scaffolding.

I kissed her after rehearsal and never told anyone.

I played the last note too long. It was the only thing that felt real.

I was more than pageantry. I was a *pulse*.

This is the sound we never gave you.

This is the chord we kept for ourselves.

This is for every time someone looked past me and called it looking at me.

This is the music of being unapplauded.

This is the fight song for the kids who will never make the highlight reel.

I was the quiet part.

I was the buildup.

I was the unresolved chord.

I was the dissonance you skipped.

I was the note that made you flinch.

I was the pause.

You wanted volume.

You got *truth.*

You wanted halftime.

This is *ours.*

You wanted background.

We were the foundation.

You wanted a show.

We gave you *ourselves.*

These are the lyrics I wrote, please go write your own, because this play now belongs to *you.*

AFTERWORD

"This one time, at band camp..."

At band camp my sophomore year my one-hundred-and-fifteen-pound frame could still barely hold up the forty-pound albatross that is the sousaphone (please note my two-handed grip). One night after dinner, Eliza (her real life equivalent, that is) put on Parliament Funkadelic's "Give Up The Funk (Tear The Roof Off The Sucker)" and it blew my face off. I named my tuba in honor of the introduction, writing "The Funk" on its bell in black electrical tape.

Thank you to the geeks and outcasts who made up my marching band.

Your friendship and bravery helped write the arc of my life.

9 780573 712302